HOME TOWN

by

Martha Baxley

PublishAmerica
Baltimore

ISBN: 1-4137-1741-1
PUBLISHED BY PUBLISHAMERICA, LLLP
www.publishamerica.com
Baltimore

Printed in the United States of America

Chapter One

LOCAL TEEN MISSING!

The headline leaped off the front page at her. Darcy gasped as she read about the quandary facing family, law enforcement, and school of the small town.

The morning had started quietly when she sighed and pushed herself away from the breakfast table. She missed Mama terribly but to dwell on her loss was less than helpful. It was better to stay busy. I can hear her voice, 'A busy person is a happy person.'

Thinking a walk in fresh air would clear her mind, she decided to check on her nearest neighbors, Clint and Nora Lassiter. But she exited her front gate just in time to wave at Clint, barreling toward his farthest field. At times she wished for more space between houses, for that exact moment Homer Hicks turned into Clint's drive to park his car out of Clint's line of vision from the field. Give Homer "A" for perfect timing! This happened often. Since Darcy was the only person in proximity to know, it made her feel guilty, as if part of a conspiracy.

Damned if I do! Damned if I don't! Clint's bound to find out sooner or later and she'll suspect I told him. That rules out popping in on Nora!

The black-eyed Susan and Indian paintbrush around her mailbox were losing ground with weeds. She busied herself there until the rural mail carrier approached. Under the battered old felt hat, Russell Banes weathered face beamed as he braked to a stop. He pushed the hat back to reveal keen blue eyes.

"Hi, young lady! You're ambitious for this early hour!"

"Thanks, Russ, for calling me a young lady. I feel ancient, with both girls married and on their own."

Laughing indulgently, Russ answered, "I pinned diapers on you! I am ancient! Darcy, do you know Aggie Brandon? She was Aggie Hayes."

"Why, yes! I do! We went through school and graduated together. She moved away when she married."

"They split up and she moved back. She and her teenage daughter live in the mobile home park in town. The daughter went missing yesterday. A state-wide bulletin is on TV and in all the papers."

He left her mail and rolled away.

Sorting as she walked to the house, SOS--same old stuff! Junk mail! she grumbled silently. But here was a letter, business-like, not from anybody she knew. H-m-m. Probably a come-on to sell something. People do anything to push their ridiculous offers, she thought, pushing it aside in favor of the daily newspaper.

The story about Aggie's daughter was front-and- center. Wow! Faith Brandon, cheerleader, in the top ten of her class. Must be like her mother. Aggie was a good student. She hastily folded the paper and hurried off to the kitchen.

While she and Ray ate lunch, she related the story of the missing girl. "Imagine Aggie's thoughts! Think how we would feel if one of ours disappeared without a trace! The story states that Faith and her mother ate supper together and talked before she retired for the night. Her mother woke next morning to find her gone, her bed not slept in! No break-in! No struggle! She just vanished! How awful!"

Ray shook his head in disbelief. "There has to be a logical explanation. She probably ran off to get married. Happens all the time. Did we get any mail?"

"That reminds me. We did get something. Probably a bill we forgot to pay."

Darcy never tired of Ray's face. As he read, she savored his Indian coloring, infectious smile that displayed his dimples, arched brows accenting golden brown eyes. Scanning the letter, Ray's tanned face quickly turned sober.

Handing it to Darcy, he said,"You should read this. It's from a lawyer who says your mother's farm has a cloud on the title."

As she carefully read the letter, her face drained of color. "Ray, I don't understand! This land was given to my family in the 1800's. The federal government forced them to give up homes, farms, everything they had, and move a thousand miles. After the grueling, miserable trek here, their misery was rewarded with raw, bare land. In spite of the treatment they received, everybody behaved and stayed out of trouble. The property tax was always paid. There was never a mortgage. How can this be?"

"It sounds like a legal hassle. We need a lawyer! A good lawyer takes money!"

Ray and Darcy dejectedly entered their home to sit in the den, staring glumly at the floor in deep shock.

Breaking the profound silence at last, Darcy burst out, "Ray, I don't understand! How was Mama hoodwinked so badly! She was intelligent and cautious to the point of being suspicious!"

"Darcy, you heard the lawyer's explanation. Mineral and oil rights were not clearly defined from right of surface ownership. It was an oversight that only a legal eagle would notice. They plan to use it to grab something that isn't theirs."

"This land belonged to my family for generations! Can someone come in now and take it away?"

"Darcy, your mother inherited allotted Indian land from her father, free of debt, mortgage or encumbrance. Now a mischance of words can affect generations."

"She read it several times! Her attorney read it! She waited several days before she signed it."

"Darcy, when a doctor gives his opinion, he may have missed an important detail. You have the right to ask another opinion. Same with a lawyer and his legal opinion. Your mother dropped the ball when she didn't do that."

"Her attorney was a lifelong friend. It would be disloyal to ask another opinion. She knew he'd resent the distrust."

"Now we must be patient while legal mills grind slowly. Courts are overloaded so we wait, maybe for two years!"

"A long time to stand with the sword of Damocles over your head!"

Chapter Two

"Hello, Aggie. It's Darcy. I read in the paper about your daughter. I called to see if I can help."

"Darcy, it's good to hear from you! Thanks for calling! Yes, I can use a friend! I'm out of my mind!"

"I'll be right there!"

She found the small mobile home on the last street at the back of the park. Aggie met her at the door to promptly burst into tears. She hugged Darcy and ushered her into the room as she chattered.

"Darcy! It's a living nightmare! I can't do anything but wait! Seems like Faith will come back any minute! You never met her so I'll show her pictures. She took ballet, a good little dancer! Wasn't she cute in her tutu? She played softball three summers and here she is in her uniform. And she won the eighth grade spelling bee! Look at that grin! She always was a good speller. This one, in her cheerleader costume, was the last taken."

Pictures were aligned in display while she nodded and made sympathetic noises in response to Aggie's babbling recital.

"She gets along well at school. Her teachers like her. She makes good grades. I tell her that grades are important because she needs a scholarship. I thought she'd sail right through highschool, go to college and then get a nice job. Where did I go wrong? She's been told, don't talk to strangers! Don't get in cars with strangers! I cannot believe my Faith could disappear completely!"

She admired the color photo of a clear-eyed all-American girl in cheerleader costume while listening to Aggie. The place was neat, clean, comfortable, definitely a home. Aggie, with slim figure, open

7

face, sprinkling of freckles, casual wind-blown hair, was a cheerleader mom.

"I don't know how you do it! You're exactly the same as when we finished highschool. Remember we voted you most like Doris Day! You've changed very little!"

Aggie let herself be drawn down memory lane. After they talked for awhile and Aggie was calmer, Darcy took her leave. A short distance from the park she passed a small, shabby camper trailer on an unkempt lot.

That's odd! I don't remember that trailer being there. I can't believe I am seeing a trailer in this area! Especially that beat-up old thing! Why here, with a mobile home park a half-mile away? I wonder someone hasn't complained and gotten it moved. What an eyesore!"

At the supper table, she related the day's event.

"Ray, we should do something for Aggie. Her husband moved away after the divorce and they never hear from him. She's a single mom with nobody to turn to and a mediocre job that barely pays the bills. An unbearable situation!"

"Darcy, did it never occur to anybody the girl ran off to get married? They should count all the boys in this town. If one is missing, go after him."

"They already tried that. It's been three months since she broke up with the kid she was dating. Ray, I know we can find a way to help to her!"

That last statement foremost in mind, Darcy sought out the sheriff next day. George Moran wasn't hard to find. George went into office on a landslide vote by his numerous relatives and in-laws scattered about the county. He and his wife were active members of the largest church in town and gave generously of money and time to many local organizations. That kept him on first-name basis with sixty-five percent of the voters. An affable, jovial person, he was always ready for a good laugh. His private policy was 'tell them a joke, treat them like folks.'

In more sober moments, he became completely involved in

business at hand, with open mind to any query. Whatever your problem, you felt that George was in your corner. On a daily basis, with very little crime in the small town, time grew heavy. When not in his office, he could be found on Main Street, handy to voters in case something came up. His tall, wide-shouldered figure and big white Stetson hat made him an easy mark.

"Hi, George! I haven't seen you since we worked on the school board election. May I buy you coffee?"

"Heck, why not? I could use it, unless it's a bribe. I'd like a good chat with you. How's Ray?"

Morton's Drug had been a focal point in the town since before Darcy was born. On the corner where the two main thoroughfares crossed, it was a natural meeting place. When the place was face-lifted, during a time when soda fountains were phased out, Jesse Morton had the gumption to retain and restyle his soda fountain and move it from the back of the store to near the front windows. People passing by could see right off if a friend was there, engaged in the town's favorite indoor sport, coffee time, and enter to sit in on any conversation. There were no secrets among friends. Jesse also had the forethought to send his only son to pharmaceutical school and then left the store to him. The whole establishment was steeped in tradition. The only drug store in town was the favorite local watering hole, the true hub, the place to keep your finger on the community pulse.

They entered to seat themselves at opposite sides of a booth. Displays of cosmetics and over-the-counter remedies all promised instant glamour or instant relief. Hiding a smile, she thought, some things never change.

George would never dream of taking his hat off. That just wasn't done, except in church. But as a concession to manners, he pushed it back off his forehead for a more casual air. For five minutes, they ceremoniously stirred coffee and chatted about local events and friends. Darcy quickly worked the conversation around to Faith Brandon. At mention of her name, George shook his head in despair.

"Darcy, it's the spookiest thing I ever heard of! That girl actually disappeared! Evidently she wore the same clothes she had on when she left her mother and went to her room. There's nothing missing except the girl and the clothes she wore. Nothing out of place, in her room or the rest of the house. She even left her purse.

"We talked to every one of their neighbors. Asked every fool question we could dream up, over and over, trying to jog somebody's memory. Nobody saw anything or heard anything. There was not a car, coming or going away. We don't know if she called someone, but the phone didn't ring all evening so nobody called her. There was no note. It's as if she simply opened the door and walked away."

"Was there trouble at school? Did she flunk a test! Kids get upset over grades. They may be at odds with a teacher but don't talk about it at home. Have you talked to her friends?"

"Of course we did! But we're dealing with an entirely different species! Kids are different from the way we were. Kids won't talk to grownups. They close down! Stare at you with blank eyes! Band together in a code of silence! Brrr! They cannot distinguish between tattling and civic duty. Seems to me they'd want to find their friend!"

"George, I worked with kids enough to know, the other kids always know! They may not share what they know with adults, but they know and they talk to each other. The kids know exactly what was going on and they will tell. Your job is to ask the right person the right question."

With a sad shake of his head, "We already tried that. It didn't work."

"Get her best friends together. Use an excuse to get them into the station. Just being there will intimidate them. Then separate them and keep them apart and alone for as long as you dare. Give them time to grow edgy, then tell each one the other gave you information. Let them stew awhile longer. Then the silence will break."

"Thanks, Darcy! You're probably right. What can we lose?"

As George walked away, Darcy saw the Tidwell twins enter the store. It would be impossible to not notice the twins. They were truly identical, giving one the impression of having double vision. They were always together. The only time they separated was the time Minnie got married. They missed each other so badly, they both cried quarts every night. Minnie divorced to return to dual existence with Mo and neither of them ever dated again. No longer young, their brown hair, now going gray around the edges, was kept in short, bunchy little curls around the face, to make them more obvious than ever. Kids pointed excitedly while exclaiming loudly, "Look, Mama! Old lady twins!"

To compound a felony, they dressed alike. Their taste was atrocious, running to bizarre fads, extreme styles, and gaudy colors in weird combinations. They could easily be seen from one end of Main Street to the other. One would stand out in a crowd. Two of a kind left most folks speechless, the teetotaler wishing for a drink and the sot ready to swear off for good.

Darcy was among the few people who remembered Mo was named Mona and always called her that. Darcy was one of the few who could tell them apart. No problem, as Minnie was half-inch taller and Mo's face a tad narrower. Another give-away was that Minnie did all the talking while Mo stood to the left, a half-step behind, chin slightly tucked, grinning and nodding in vigorous agreement with every word Minnie uttered. They liked to sing, mostly nasal renditions of gospel songs, and would sing at the drop of a hat.

"Hello, Mona! Minnie! I'm glad to see you! We don't see each other often enough. I see you have your guitar, Minnie. Do you still play?"

"We go to the nursing home each week. It's pure pleasure for us to see the way those people enjoy our gospel songs."

"Ray, does it seem odd that oil lease went unnoticed until Mama was gone? It should have turned up sooner. Why now, when Mama's not here to give testimony? Even worse, her attorney is gone. Why now?"

"You have a point. Maybe someone knew about the lease with faulty wording and held on to it until she was gone. Question—who's in a position to do that?"

"At the time there was talk of drilling that spread like wildfire.

Everybody got excited, thinking we could have an oil field here. Then, suddenly as it began, it faded away and nothing ever came of it. Except that Mama got the lease money. We were in a drouth so she was glad to get it."

"Do you remember the name of the oil company? What happened to the company? It would be helpful to check their records."

"I was little more than a baby when it happened. But I know I'm a simple country girl and I'm out of my league. We need help. We need a private detective."

Chapter Three

The old man drove slowly, almost absent-mindedly, along the country road. His memories of that road were dust in dry weather, mire when it rained. Now it was all-weather and straighter. Hmm! That farm was different, with the old barn replaced by a new one. He shook his head ruefully, thinking, farmers will opt to build a new barn and continue to live in an ancient house!

The cemetery, begun on a hilltop away from the road, had grown to reach the lane. The elegant new entry gate added a nice touch. Remembering a favorite quote, 'certain as death and taxes' brought another doleful shake of the head. The church nearby remained unchanged. And there was the Lassiter house! He remembered them as good neighbors, helpful when needed but inclined to tend to their own affairs. Wonder if they still lived there?

At the next house he stopped near the front gate to sit stock still and stare about in avid curiosity. Hmm! Looked like the old gal kept the place in good repair. The house, though basically the same, was newly painted with flowers blooming near the door. Around the well-kept lawn ran an expensive new fence. It set off that fine old house like pearls on a beautiful woman's neck.

Tall crepe myrtle lined the back fence, screening barn and outbuildings from the house. Gentle wind wafted the blooming shrubs to sway rhythmically. He found that soothing. He nodded his approval of the big pecan trees that kept the place cool in hot weather. A central air unit beside the house got another vote. Those trees could use a little help during a heat wave. The new double garage at the side showed one empty space and a late-model car. With an experienced eye, he noted the cattle in the pasture were of good quality stock. We-e-ell, she hadn't done too badly! A good place to spend one's retirement, he thought complacently.

He stepped out of the car, adjusted his Western hat to a jaunty angle, and squared his shoulders. He made his way up the steps and knocked confidently. A pretty woman with auburn hair and dark eyes opened the door to stare in obvious curiosity.

"Sarah?"

"Oh, you must want my mother. I'm Darcy."

"The hair should have tipped me off. You were a redhead from the start but you do resemble her. I want to see Sarah."

"She isn't here. Are you an old friend ?"

"Anne? Augusta?"

"They don't live here."

"I've driven a long way. I've traveled too far to make a pop call. I would like to come in."

They stared at each other in obvious curiosity, the old man and the younger woman. Uninvited strangers did not enter her house, yet there was about him a familiar quality. Despite his age, he was a strikingly handsome man. Flashing ebony eyes riveting on her commanded attention. Memory stirred. He reminded her of something, someone.

His air of confidence won out. She obligingly opened the door and stood aside. Without pause, he strode confidently toward the den to seat himself in Ray's large easy chair. Exuding pleasure, he looked about possessively, like a king on his throne.

He observed shelves filled with books, fine old polished family heirlooms, wood paneling complemented with an expanse of gold carpet. He gazed out a bank of windows at flowers and wide-spreading trees. He stared about at everything, like a thirsty man greedily drinking from an oasis.

At last he spoke. "Now tell me why I cannot see Sarah? As I said, I have driven a long way."

"We lost my mother three months ago. She had cancer and there was nothing anyone could do," Darcy told him with trembling lips.

He bowed his head for a speechless moment. "I waited too long," with a sad shake of his head. "I should have come when I first began thinking of it. For that, I am truly sorry! Tell me about Augusta and Ann. "

"Augusta lives in the next county. Ann lives in California. Both are well. You have the advantage. Evidently you know my family but I don't know you."

He sat poised in obvious anticipation while Darcy wavered. The face was only vaguely familiar but the voice awoke something in her. It was like trying to recall a dream. His black eyes riveted into her inner self and drew her like magnets, making it impossible to look away.

"Darcy, I am your father. I am James Shannon."

A moment of shocked silence before she burst out, "That's impossible! My father is dead! He died when I was a baby!"

"Darcy, did Sarah and the girls tell you I was dead?"

Another long thoughtful silence before she admitted grudgingly, "Actually, no! I always supposed you were dead so I never asked. On the other side of the coin, they never mentioned your name. Even more reason to believe you were dead. My mother never told me anything about my father and I never asked! We were a family and we got along fine! But I never had a father! I have every right to ask, where were you all the years I grew up without a father?"

"I will tell you but it's a long story. I had rather not get into it today. I am a tired old man, too tired to talk!"

"You must be thirsty," She excused herself and went to the kitchen.

Ray chose that moment to leave his work and enter the house. Seeing the older man seated in his chair, he smiled and strode across the room to offer his hand.

"I'm Ray Parker."

"James Shannon."

"You must be related to Darcy. Have you traveled far?"

"Yes, to both questions," he laughed.

Darcy returned with three mugs of coffee and seated herself beside Ray. Taking a deep breath, she broke the awkward silence.

"Ray, have you met my father?"

The older man offered his hand again. Ray sat gaping while the stranger grinned, enjoying the obvious shock like a small boy with a prank. Withdrawing his wallet from his pocket, he said, "My driver license. My birth certificate, along with my army discharge, is among my things in the car. I have no doubt about you, Darcy. You're the image of my Irish grandmother, most especially the hair."

Darcy, near tears, blurted, "Why did you wait so long to appear? All those years I needed a father and never had one! After so many years, why bother to come back now?"

"Darcy, it's a long story. I cannot tell you now. It would take too long and I am too tired to talk. Is there some place I may rest awhile? I'm exhausted. I would like to lie down."

After they had shown the old man to the spare room, even brought in some of his things from his car, he promptly fell into deep slumber. Ray and Darcy returned to the den to sit in stunned silence.

"I cannot believe this! All my life I thought I had no father. Mama never mentioned him so I never asked. There were no pictures of him, never any mention of his name! I thought she missed him so much, she couldn't talk about him. All that time, he never wrote or called!"

"You don't know that. If your mother would not discuss him, would she mention a call or a letter?"

Snapping his fingers in sudden thought, "Darcy, we took a total stranger into our home! A man shows up out of thin air and we immediately take him in, give him the spare room, and never asked to see his papers! Are we a couple of chumps?"

"Ray, I knew him the minute I saw him! A clear case of deja vu! He asked for my mother and sisters by name! You should have seen the way he walked into this house! He pranced in here like a hero returning from the wars! He knew exactly where he was! I can hardly wait to hear his version. Ray, I know he is my father! It's his eyes! My eyes are exactly like his! Now that is spooky!"

She burst into laughter. " I can hardly wait to tell Gussie and Ann our father has risen from the dead!"

Chapter Four

After a hearty breakfast, James Shannon finished off his third cup of coffee with a flourish. Giving Darcy a glowing look of approval, he observed, "Young lady, you're as good a cook as your mother! I haven't enjoyed a meal like that in ages! It's like coming home!"

"Speaking of—we're waiting to hear your story; where you have been, and why you lived apart from your family. Curiosity grows by the minute. It may get the best of me."

"We'll get to that eventually. Right now I want to go with Ray to see your herd. It's a treat to walk about the pasture and discuss cattle and crops with a true cattleman! Come on, Ray! Let's go! We're burning daylight!" he commanded. He jammed his hat on his head and marched out the back door to Ray's pickup to seat himself and wait imperiously.

"I give him high marks for making himself right at home," Ray muttered as he reached for his hat and followed.

Over lunch, as the three again faced each other at the table, Darcy asked,"How long do you plan to be here, James? Do you want to call Ann and Gussie? Shall we plan a full-scale visit here or would you rather contact each at home? I can ask Anne to fly home. Or you may rather travel to the West Coast. I'm waiting to hear your story."

Drily he retorted, "Darcy, there is no hurry for my story, as you insist on calling it. It's taken a lifetime to live it. I'll discuss it when I'm ready. Right now it feels good to be home! It still feels like home! I didn't realize how I missed this place! Never realized how tired I was til I got here. After a few days rest I will talk. I'll contact

17

my other daughters when I feel like it."

"Would you like to visit Mama's grave?"

"I don't lurk around graveyards but for Sarah, I'll make an exception. Is she in the cemetery here? In the family plot?"

"Of course."

"I'll find it," he said as he left the house.

Darcy answered the phone to hear the sheriff say, "Darcy, I have something to tell. Stop when you're in town."

"I can't wait! I'll be right there."

"I'll be in the park across the street from my office."

"Have a seat, Darcy. Shame to waste perfect weather. My office is an ant bed! It's more private out here. I want to thank you for steering me right with those kids. It worked!"

"George, kids haven't changed much. It takes longer to find the right button to push on some of them. Now tell!"

"We asked Faith Brandon's two best friends to come down and look at pictures. We asked them to identify anybody they saw around the school or with Faith. I had to wait til the right time. I find out a lot by hanging around the drug store. I knew their fathers planned to attend an auction for registered bulls. We saw the men leave town together and we knew their wives went to the city for an all-day shopping spree. We went to the school and asked the girls to come to the station. We had all day to work with them.

"We put them in separate rooms to look at mug shots, told them they could work better without distraction. We told them we had to be sure that one opinion wasn't influenced by the other. We left them there as long as we dared before we told each one the other gave information we could use. It worked! They both told us that in the last three months, Faith had gotten into drugs and was dating her supplier but she didn't want her mother to know. She thought she could get herself out of it but she wasn't doing a very good job of it. Then they clammed up, wouldn't give us a name, description, or anything else."

18

"They may suspect, or they may know but are afraid to tell. You may get more from them later."

"I hate my job when I get into things like this! How can I tell Aggie? A nice clean kid like Faith Brandon on drugs! Her mother will never believe it!"

Darcy took the long way home to detour past the mobile home park. She knew Aggie was at work but something nagged her. It picked at the back of her mind every time she thought about that camper trailer. If she could get the right cue, she might remember. As she passed the shabby camper a short distance from the mobile home park, she again shook her head in disbelief. When she saw the expensive car parked nearby, her first thought was, I cannot imagine driving a Jaguar while living in that rat trap! There's no accounting for taste! was her disgusted thought.

"Darcy, that private detective called while you were out. He rooted out something we need but he won't discuss it by phone. He asked us to come by his office soon as possible."

"How soon can we go?"

"Tomorrow. This is priority for both of us."

Once again they sat in their home, downcast, sad, dejected. At last, Darcy broke the long silence. "Ray, this is the worst possible scenario! Giving up Mama was the hardest thing I ever had to do!

"Then it was another nightmare when her will was read. I had no idea she left the family farm to me! I was as surprised as everybody else. It was a dreadful shock when Gussie flew into a rage and turned on me. She acted like I used my influence to sway Mama's decision. Mama plainly stated in her will that she did not want the farm divided. Like others before her, she said the one who would tend it and pass it on intact should be the receiver, the caretaker. I'm only a custodian but Gussie doesn't feel that way.

"Mama left money for Gussie and Anne because she knew Anne wouldn't wipe her feet on the place. She prefers the "Bright Lights." Gussie has no intention to live here. She wanted 'her share' so she

19

could sell it and give the money to her kids. Sell this ranch, property that has been in our family for one hundred and fifty years! Mama knew all of that.

"This entire past year has been one shock after another. I grieve for Mama and I grieve because I lost Mama and Gussie at the same time."

"Your mother was right! You do care about this place. A son would be the obvious choice but with no male heir, you were the logical one."

"This place was special to me as a child. I love it even more since I'm old enough to appreciate the history and sentimental value. I agree with Mama. To chop it up is wanton destruction. In three generations, it will be truck farms!"

"I hope we don't get thrown out of here! We can always go back to our own place but we have gone to a considerable amount of labor and expense to close our own place and move here. We spent even more adapting it to our taste. That's not the point. It's rightfully ours and we should not be thrown off our own place! That detective gave us more hope than anyone else. After his explanation, it's easier to understand."

"Can you imagine someone we trusted without question? I would have trusted that banker with our life savings! That is exactly what we did! Fred Jenson is a sly devil, planning for years to steal our land! All the while he shook hands with us, patted us on the back, and acted like he was sorry Mama was gone!"

"That oil lease is a public record. We didn't know where to look but the detective traced it with no problem. When the person holding it offered it as collateral for a bank loan, Jenson was shrewd enough to make him an attractive offer and buy it outright. Most leases expire after a stated date but the wrong wording left it open. He plans to grab prime real estate, plus all mineral interest, for what he paid for the lease. Pretty neat profit!"

"I hope the judge shares our view."

James poked his head into the kitchen for a cautious look around.

Seeing only Darcy, busy at the sink, he came in to pour coffee and seat himself at the kitchen table. After a profound silence and a measuring gaze at his daughter, he spoke abruptly.

"Darcy, we don't know each other very well, but you are my daughter. You have a problem and I want to help. I couldn't help overhearing the conversation between you and Ray, about the lawsuit against your land. I can end it before it ever comes to trial."

"James, I don't know you well enough to call you 'Daddy' so I'll call you James. You eavesdropped to hear something private. You overheard something you have no business knowing. I want you to leave it at that! It is not your concern! Keep the information to yourself!"

"I woke up from a sound sleep to hear every word you said. But you don't need to worry about me. I can keep my mouth shut. My father taught me one principle of good health. He said it should be the eleventh commandment--"Breathe through thy nose." I will pass that philosophy on to you. The less other folks know about your business, the better for you."

"That's interesting! I know very little about your side of the family and I do want to hear more. We could spend hours with family history."

"You should be more patient with your elders. I'm not ready to spill my guts. I don't repeat myself so I'll talk when I get my story straight. Now I have something else I want to discuss. I'll tell this to you and you must never repeat it, to Ray, to anyone! I can get rid of that crooked banker! Say the word and all your troubles will go away!"

"Good Lord! Are you saying what I think you are saying? This is terrible!"

"Terrible! I'll tell you what's terrible! Losing your family farm through no fault of your own is terrible! That crook will steal your land if you don't protect yourself!"

"James, I wont even think about the monstrous thing you speak of! I wish I never had this conversation!"

"Keep it to yourself, Girlie! Tell and you implicate yourself!"

Chapter Five

"Hello, Aggie. Any progress in finding your daughter?"

"Darcy, waiting is awful! I know it's only a couple of days to most folks but it seems like a year to me! I can't sleep! I walk around in a daze! This place is so quiet it gives me the creeps! I can't wait to get out of here and go to work. Then I go out of my mind at work, thinking she might call while I'm out!"

"Aggie, I have to come into town for errands later. May I come by for a few minutes before bedtime?"

"I'd be grateful for someone to talk to! It's all bad but early evening is the worst time for me!"

"Come in, Darcy! I have fresh coffee and a pan of brownies just out of the oven. Faith likes brownies. It helps to have something on hand, in case she walks in. Let's sit down and have a nice talk. How's Ray? Tell me about your daughters. I heard they are both married."

"Yes, they married and moved away. The husbands have fantastic jobs and they're involved and busy. We see them at Christmas and Mothers Day. Otherwise, it's Email and phone calls."

"Ray, when I left Aggie's, a big construction site is on my usual path so I took a different route out of town. I went around to the east side of town, out by the service station on the highway, Marv's Mini Mart, it's called. Since it was past most folks' bedtime, houses were dark, absolutely no traffic. Then I passed the "Y" where the street meets the highway.

"After business hours, the station is closed but a collection of

23

cars was parked there. No lights, nothing going on. A crowd of teenage boys in small groups. They were smoking, lolling, leaning on cars, just killing time. Why are all those kids out there this time of night?"

"Darcy, kids never want to go to bed when the grownups do. There is usually a dance or ball game on weekends but week nights, you could fire a shot down Main Street and not hit a soul. There is nothing to do on week nights. You know how kids are. If there is nothing going on, they will find something to get into."

"I know all that and it bothers me. There were fifteen or twenty boys hanging around there. What could they get into on the dark parking lot of a closed service station?"

Chapter Six

Darcy answered the phone to hear Ann's voice.

"Hello, Baby Sister! How's life in the boondocks? Does anything ever happen there?"

"Ann! I've been waiting for your call! I hope you're sitting down because something has happened! Ann, our father is here!"

After a long silence, "Did you say our father is there?"

"He arrived here unannounced, late one afternoon, and knocked on my door. He says he wants to see you and Gussie but puts it off day to day. He makes a fine art of procrastination. Anne, I thought he was dead! Why did nobody ever tell me the truth?"

"When he dropped completely out of sight, we could only suppose something happened to him and he would never be back. If we mentioned him, we would have to tell all of it. You were so young when he left, it seemed unwise to try to tell you then. When you were old enough to hear the story, it had been so long, we thought he was dead. We talked it over and felt it best to never mention it. Gussie and I can remember him but we also remember the bad along with the good. We had trouble feeling any pride in the fact that he was our father. We were secretly glad when he left. It was good riddance!"

"Gussie and I are not on good terms right now. Remember, she went into one of her snits the day Mama's will was read? It still goes on. I would call her but when she's in one of her humors, she alters between disagreeable and judgmental.

"Now James is here and has an attitude of 'The conquering hero returns.' He's in my spare room, with run of the place. When I ask his plans, he only talks about how good it is to be back home. He acts like he may be ill. I don't want to be mean or hateful to a sick old man but I wish somebody would tell me the truth! He says he will but only when he feels like it! Lord only knows when the mood will strike him! Anne, was he in trouble when he left?"

"Darcy, he was always in trouble! That's all I will say until he has a chance to tell his version. Then you may check with me for verification. I was just a kid when he left. I'm sure I didn't know all of it but I remember more than I want to."

"I have more news! We have a lawsuit on our hands! Someone is trying to take away our family farm. An old oil lease has come to light. Like the bad fairy, it has come out of the past and will not go away. We have much to talk about."

"That won't be for months."

"Do you plan a visit?"

"I have to work for a living, you know! I don't get my vacation until later in the year. He left with no forwarding address! He took his own sweet time about contacting any of us! I certainly won't extend myself to see him! If he wants to see me, he can travel out here!"

Chapter Seven

"Hello"

"Darcy, this is George. I have a big favor to ask. I can't ask just anybody to do this. You are the only one I know who can handle this."

"Good Lord, George! I'm ready to hang up! This must be something nobody in his right mind would do!"

"Darcy, you know I have to handle every kind of problem you can imagine. Remember last year, when that bad wreck happened east of town? When Toby Haines was driving too fast and ran off the pavement. Then he tried to drive back onto the pavement. They always do that and it's always a fatal mistake. He over-corrected, hit an eighteen-wheeler head-on. Killed him and his wife but the truck driver wasn't even scratched. Remember that?"

"How could I forget? The whole town was in shock and mourning for days. What has that to do with me now? "

"Darcy, remember they left a daughter? She's about fourteen. We put her in foster care because there was no close relative. All we could locate were a couple of distant cousins too old to cope. When we told her about them, she begged to stay here. She didn't want to change schools or move away. She said it was bad enough that she lost her parents. It wasn't right to take away her school and community, too. So we put her in foster care. Now the foster parents asked to have her placed in another home. Could you take her for a few days? Do me a favor and help the kid til we find another place? She's a nice quiet kid who needs a place to stay. You are the obvious one to ask, for I know how well your own kids turned out. I remember all those honors and scholarships they won!"

"George, you can stop the sweet talk and big compliments. I know when I am being brain washed! The poor girl shouldn't feel like a stray puppy. Of course I'll take her! How much trouble can one little girl be?"

Grace Coombs, director of foster care, was brisk and business-like. Slim and trim, she dressed in a professional style to add to her reputation for getting things done, which she took great pride in. Another thing most people remembered about Grace was her eyes, pea green like shiny emeralds. She was proud of those eyes and usually wore something to make them more notable. Darcy noticed that today it was a green scarf at her neck. The girl beside her resembled a young colt, long limbs and big brown eyes, scared and wary.

Grace smiled as she chirped, "Darcy, this is Gaylene Haines. I know you two remember each other. Now, I'll get out of the middle and let you get acquainted."

"Thank you, Grace. Hello, Gaylene. We're glad to have you. Come in! Let me show you around the house and then we will look at your room."

After a brief tour of the house, Darcy helped Gaylene place her things in the small bedroom at the end of the hall.

"I hope you like blue," she laughed as she threw open the door. "This was Jenny's room and she is a fiend for blue."

Gaylene gazed about at antique furniture painted white, white spread, ruffled white curtains, pale blue-gray carpet, all accented by sky blue walls. The large window looked out on the same view as the den, a large, old-fashioned porch and a shielded area of flowers, shrubs, birdbath and bird feeder under a large pecan tree. A little corner of Eden. As she took it all in, her face brightened and some of the uncertainty left her eyes.

"The student desk is okay for homework. The small rocker was my mother's. I hope you will feel at home."

She led the way to the kitchen and placed a plate of cookies and a couple of soft drinks on the kitchen table.

"Let's have a snack to hold us until supper while we get better acquainted," Darcy suggested.

Gayene got a glass of water for herself and chose a chair across from Darcy. She gazed inquisitively about the kitchen. Though the house was of a different vintage, the kitchen met present standards with new appliances. Pale yellow walls and sheer white curtains gave a sunny aura, even on dark days. A small table and chairs at the window gave them a broad view of clear sky and rolling prairie covered with native flowers.

She answered Darcy's questions politely as she drank an occasional sip of water. Darcy deliberately ate a couple of cookies and drank her coke.

"I'm sorry I don't have your flavor. What kind of pop do you like? What's your favorite cookie?"

"I don't eat sweets often," was the reply.

"You must go grocery shopping with me and show me what you like. Ray and I are democratic in food tastes. That means we eat anything that doesn't bite us first. You must alert me about dislikes or allergies. We are flexible."

She was rewarded with a noncommittal Mona Lisa smile. I feel like I am having this conversation with myself, she thought ruefully.

"It's nice to have enough people at this table to keep a conversation going," Darcy remarked at the supper table. "Ray and I rattle around in this place, never make enough noise to scare the mice. James, Gaylene will be staying with us for awhile. Gaylene, my father, James Shannon. How nice! Three generations at the table! We can share a cross-poll of opinion."

Throughout the meal, the three generations shared total silence, broken only by the noise of dishes and silver in use. Gaylene smiled her little Mon Lisa smile while James busied himself with seriously attending his plate and passing serving dishes.

To help pave the way, Ray chimed in. "We don't mean to be nosy, Gaylene. We knew your parents well and we want to get acquainted with you. We know you'll be more comfortable when you don't feel like a stranger."

Through all the fuss over her, Gaylene smiled and toyed with a small amount of food on her plate. Pleading homework, she soon excused herself to retire to her room.

"Ah, yes, homework! Plus the school bus early every morning, ball games, practice periods, shopping, dental appointments, hair appointments! Darcy, are you sure you want back into the kid business?"

"Ray, I know this is a bolt of lightning! I didn't have time to ponder on it. The child needed a home so I followed my heart. I miss our girls and it's good to feel needed once more. I have time on my hands since I left the classroom so I see no problem. She's well-behaved, makes good grades, and she's fifteen. It won't last forever."

"I understand. I also understand who will do all the work, parent-teacher stuff, lunch money, the right clothes. She is old enough to be interested in boys. Remember boys? Boys with cars? Scrapes our girls got into? Their choice of friends?"

"Of course I do! Ray, through the years your routine has changed very little. I left the classroom when the girls finished college. Now I have time on my hands. I like to bake and I'm a whiz with decorated birthday cakes and wedding cakes. I thought about custom baking but living out in the country makes it awkward. So I have big plans to make this place into a bed-and-breakfast inn. Think about it, Ray! I can put up a nice sign on the highway and before you know it, I'll have two or three couples in here every night!"

Ray laughed. "Okay! Okay! I give up! I'm on the ropes! Strangers in my house every night is not an option. But this may not be a cakewalk!"

Chapter Eight

"Darcy, this is George. How are you getting along with Gaylene?"

"She's spends most of her time in her room. I took her shopping but that was a waste of time! She's not one bit interested in clothes. I never saw a girl refuse clothes! I would like to get her into a hobby but we have to find the right one. She says she has homework and she reads. We put a TV in her room. Thought our choice of programs turned her off. I hope, when we are better acquainted, we can get her out more."

"Darcy, I'm glad it's working but that's not why I called. I need help with something else. Aren't you friendly with Aggie Brandon?"

"Yes. I stopped a few times to spend time. She needs a friend, someone she can talk to."

"Darcy, will you meet me at her place in an hour? I have something to tell her and she needs someone with her."

Darcy hung up the phone and turned to James. "Ray has gone for the day so it's just you and me for lunch. I have to go to a friends' house. If I am not back when you get hungry, a plate is ready for you in the fridge. Pop it into the microwave and make yourself at home. This may take awhile. I don't know when I will be back."

She arrived at Aggie's small mobile home to find nobody there. But instantly Aggie drove in beside her, smiling her bright smile as she waved.

"Hi, Darcy! George called me at work and said to meet him here! I'm glad you're here, too. Now let's go in and put the coffee on. He said he has something to tell me. I was sure he would find her! I wonder where she slipped off to!"

But as they climbed the steps, the sheriff's car rolled in. He quickly joined them and as they entered the small home, he spoke.

"Aggie, please sit down. I must tell you something."

Aggie seated herself on the edge of a dining chair with an air of expectancy, eyes shining bright like a kid waiting for Santa Claus.

"Aggie, tell me once more. Exactly what did Faith wear that last day? There has been a discovery that we take seriously. A body was found, the body of a young girl."

"No! No! Don't tell me this! It can't be her!"

Kindly but firmly, George spoke."Aggie, we have to go there! It's the only lead we have and we have to exhaust every channel. The description fits: sex, weight, age, even the hair. We have to do this!"

With frozen face, Aggie stared at the floor while numbly listing Faith's clothing and her dentist. But as the sheriff drove away, she collapsed on the sofa to dissolve into tears.

Darcy decided this was a good time to put the coffee on. Then she sat down beside Aggie and offered one of Ray's clean handkerchiefs. Tissue was fine most of the time but for tears of this magnitude, a handkerchief was needed. Since nobody can cry forever, Darcy let her cry until she finished with the first harsh onslaught of anguish. As she tapered to sniffling and wiping tears, Darcy spoke.

"Aggie, there is nothing anyone can say to make this easier. Would you like to lie down and rest awhile?"

The words brought on a fit of shivering. "No! No! I don't want to be alone! Not with all those awful thoughts whirling around in my head! When George said 'body,' a cold chill went through me. Br-r-r! I am still cold! All this time I told myself she went off to think, maybe about who to date. I hated it when she broke up with that nice boy. I tried to talk to her about that but she changed the subject every time I tried.

"She hasn't been herself lately. She's always happy, making funny remarks that keep us giggling. Lately she was too quiet, like she was sick and didn't want to talk about it. We just scrape by but I told her, 'Don't worry, we can work it out.'

"When she left, I thought maybe she went to find work! But she's only sixteen! She couldn't find much to do but flip burgers. Pour us some coffee, Darcy, and stay with me. Please don't leave me alone! I pray it's a false alarm! I know it's someone's daughter but I only have one! I hope to God, not mine!"

"Ray, it's been two weeks. This is the first lead and there are too many similarities. I'm positive it is Faith and my heart breaks for Aggie. One child and now that child is snatched away!"

"Darcy, none of this makes sense. Did George tell you where this girl was found or how she was found?"

"He was discreet, trying to spare Aggie. Also he knew the slightest hint would bring out the media. They do get in the way! They try to make themselves important by guesswork and blowing up minor details. He can't say much. Gossip flies around this town worse than leaves in a high wind. He has to be quiet until he knows for sure. He would rather Aggie hear it from him than from a clumsy neighbor. When George has more exact information, he will give a full report to the media so people can get it straight."

"How do you get along with Gaylene?"

Darcy shrugged as she told him, "I hardly know the girl is here. Have you noticed the way she picks and plays with her food and leaves most of it on her plate? It's like feeding a sick cat! She moves around like a cat, with little to say for herself. Most teenage girls do their nails and chatter. They read fashion magazines. They talk about boys and clothes. She has to be the quietest girl I ever saw! I have taken a ghost into my house!"

"Let's hope she warms up to us later. Her parents sudden death was a shock for her. One day everything was right. Next, she was in foster care with total strangers. There could have been a conflict of personalities there. Has James gotten a notion to talk?"

"I'm stranded with two mummies! That man plays his cards close to his vest. He's old with no visible means of support and no place to live. I think he came here because he has no place to go. He may be like the 'street people' we read about, living in their cars and moving about to avoid the law. I believe he came back with every intention of living out his days here with Mama. If my mother were alive, he would ask her to take him back. I amend that to read—he would never stoop to ask. The man has the nerve of a government mule! He would march in to announce that he was home to stay. Then convince her how lucky she was! He's just about done that with us. I think we have him to care for. How do you feel about that?"

"There are no limits on parenthood. Kids stay eighteen years but parents can stay until called to the Great Beyond. Gaylene will be here three years. The good Lord only knows how long James can last. How do you feel about that?"

"I know nothing about the man. Mama would not have three children with him unless he had worthwhile qualities. I have watched carefully, to find he has many. To list a few, no bad habits like drinking or smoking. He's clean, well-groomed, good table manners, good grammar, quiet but pleasant company. Yet he is very entertaining when he chooses to be. A real spellbinder when the mood strikes him. He and Mama were teachers when they met, so he's educated. Add intelligent and charming.

"This leaves me torn. Where was he when we all needed a father? My mother raised the three of us with no help at all. In bad times she struggled to keep us clothed and in school. There is always a lack in an all-female atmosphere. There were times I needed the support and steady influence of a good father.

"He wanders in after a lifetime of nothing, after years of dodging responsibility. Do I take him in as the long-lost father he claims to be or do I toss him out as a lousy, deserting, absentee parent?"

Chapter Nine

"Girlie, tell me about this fuss over the land title. I haven't heard much about it lately. Did that slick banker back off?"

"No, James. A legal matter is extremely slow, a wearing, tedious process. We must keep a wait-and-see attitude."

"I can take care of it so it never comes to court. Just say the word."

"If I did that, I would be guilty of something. I think it is called 'aiding and abetting.' Something I don't want on my conscience the rest of my life."

"If a thing needs doing, you don't dawdle! You attend it with dispatch! I did a hitch in the army during wartime. Then I did a stretch in the state prison. Nobody there had a conscience. They couldn't afford one if they aimed to survive! I can handle this! Just say the word!"

"How long were you in the army?"

"Couple of years. I was an officer in the artillery. I got along fine because I was firm but fair with my men. I never ordered them to do things I was too cowardly to do. I did not issue orders from behind a desk or a barricade. I led my men and I was proud to do it."

"Was that after you left here?"

"No. It was when I was a young man. I left here to serve time and your mother asked me to not come back. She was fed up with me. The land was hers so I had no stake in it. Everybody we knew thought I married her for her land but that wasn't so.

"We were young teachers in the same school when we met. She was a beautiful woman and we met, we dated, and we grew to love one another. I asked her to marry me before I knew about her land. After we planned marriage, she told me that someday she would have a section of prime ranch land.

"I couldn't see that hurt a thing. She owned the land but she needed a man to handle it. I'm a farm boy. Country life never gave me a problem. I had a beautiful woman and a prime farm, all in one bundle. I considered that a stroke of very good fortune. I loved her from the time we met but I never bothered to tell the neighbors that. It really wasn't their concern. Figured they wouldn't believe me, so why bother?"

"What about your prison time?"

"Nothing dramatic like the stories you read in the papers, about gangsters, racketeers, drug dealers. I never could leave women alone! I don't know if it's a bad habit or just something that comes with the genes. With me, it became a game, then an obsession. I would truly try to behave. Then one day I'd see a woman and it would go all over me, like a rash. I would go chasing after her like a hound after a rabbit. I could have used more sense! I made people mad at me–a lot of people I should have kept on my side. Some men never forgive you for fooling around with their wife. They take it personally.

"I was brought in on a bogus charge. It should have been dropped for lack of evidence but I had made a state senator mad at me. The local sheriff and the county attorney were ready to shoot me on sight for getting cosy with their women. They couldn't prove I was in the wrong bed but they could stack the jury against me like a crooked gambler stacks his cards. They meant to get rid of me.

"So I was tried and convicted, not of the original charge but for grazing in the wrong pasture. The day I left for the state prison at McAlester, Sarah told me to not come back. She was a quiet woman but when she spoke, it was to the point. She said she was sick of me and fed up with my dirty tricks. Can't say I blame her. I went to prison expecting to stay awhile. I was sentenced to two years but was out in only a few months on good behavior."

"Did you try to see us?"

"No. By then, I had time to think about the events leading to the trial. I could see why she said those things to me. The enormity of my vice was so overwhelming, I could not face her. I had plenty of time to think about how I threw my family away for foolish whims.

"Then, too, I knew the neighbors would never let it rest. It's the nature of the human beast. Every time I passed someone's house or met them on the street, they would bring up the past, whisper, point, talk about it in front of their kids until it was on my kids like slime- - 'Your daddy did time! Your daddy's a jailbird!'

"I've seen the cruel ways of kids on the playground. Or in the bathroom when the teacher isn't around. I made the decision that I couldn't do that to my kids. It seemed a good idea to let it all die down. I would rather my kids remember me for something good or not at all. I took my parole and went to Alaska. Now if you don't mind, I'll stretch out for awhile. I tire easily lately. All this talking leaves me drained. I am exhausted."

With all the dignity he could muster, he rose to make his way slowly toward his room.

Chapter Ten

"Gaylene, I'm making cookies today. It's raining, it's Saturday, and I find cookies are always fun. They're even more fun as a project. I would like your company.

"Yes, ma'am. I never made cookies. I don't know what to do."

"First, we read the recipe and check to see if we have all the right ingredients. Then we divide the tasks. Do you like chocolate chip cookies?"

"They are okay, I guess. I don't eat sweets."

"Tie this apron around your waist. I'll turn on the oven so it will be hot when we need it. Here's a mixing bowl and a spoon. I'll measure while you stir."

Darcy bustled and chattered. As they greased pans, stirred, measured, they made a companionable amount of clatter. As they progressed with the task, they began to talk. Or Darcy talked while Gaylene nodded and made agreeable little sounds. They were placing spoonfuls of dough on cookie sheets in a moment of companionable silence when Darcy asked,

"Do you know Faith Brandon? Is she in your grade at school?"

"She's a junior. I am a sophomore. I see her at school but we move in different circles."

Wow! Three sentences! Three complete declarative sentences in one breath! I feel like I just broke the sound barrier! thought Darcy.

"What is Faith into at school?"

"She is a cheerleader."

"Anything else?"

"She's on the honor roll. She dates."

"Who does she date? Anyone particular boy?"

"She dated a boy named Paul. For awhile." A shrug and a shake of the head. "They broke up."

"Was it Faith or Paul who wanted to break up?"

"Don't know. I heard they had a big fight and then broke up."

"Does she date anybody else?"

"I saw her in a red Jaguar once,"Gaylene avowed and receded into her inner self as she continued to place little wads of dough on cookie sheets.

"George, on a wild guess, how many red Jaguars are in this town?"

"Darcy, if you want to play twenty questions, you'll have to do better than that. I know of one. I haven't been properly introduced to the boy but I see him around. Why do you ask?"

"I heard that Faith Brandon was seen riding in that car. Does that clear up anything for you?"

George's eyebrows went up."Maybe. I need more information before I can legally stop somebody and shake him down. But it may point me in the right direction."

Chapter Eleven

"Ray, have you heard about the special election? Jim Nance applied for a license to open a liquor store here. Now he is facing a big hurdle. A local law forbids sale of liquor in our town. Within the city limits, to be exact. The townspeople are discussing the possibility but, of course, they will all take sides. Now a big fight is brewing between the drys and the wets."

"Passing a law against the sale of liquor was pure folly in the first place. You cannot enforce the way people behave in their homes. The people who want to drink can buy all the liquor they want across the state line, take it home, and drink til they pop. Just remember what Will Rogers said. 'Oklahoma will stay dry as long as the voters can stagger to the polls.'"

"That held true until the state voted to go wet with county and city options. That means it will get personal in a hurry. It could turn into civil war. Just when it looked like we could all get along with one another," Darcy mourned.

"It hasn't even warmed up yet. Next the preachers will get into it. They take full advantage of a pulpit and a congregation. They cannot resist a captive audience. Then the local editor takes his stance. This would be a good time to leave town for an extended trip."

"Hah! You talk a good game! You wouldn't miss this for all the tea in China! This could turn into another version of 'The Hatfields and McCoys.' Many of our families have intermarried until they can hardly remember who is related and who is in-law. We have as many as three siblings of one family married to three siblings of another family. This may improve their memory, all for the worse," she mourned.

"It may bring back more than we all can handle. We haven't completely recovered from that strange school board election. You remember, the one that involved the death of a former mayor?"

"A nightmare! People lost site of the original purpose of the election. There were people who voted only to use their vote as a weapon to even old scores."

"People in small towns have long memories."

Darcy stopped in the midst of errands to buttonhole George Moran. "Hello, George. Have coffee with me?"

"Sure, Darcy. A quick cup. Let's step into Morton's Drug."

As they stirred, "Darcy, have you heard about Joe Lipton?"

"Your deputy? Not a word."

"Don't tell anybody else! I had to fire that idiot!"

"Do you want to add anything to that?"

"He needed a job and I needed a deputy! He was my only applicant or I would never have hired him. I knew he had a bad habit of chasing women. If a woman happens to cross his line of vision, she is fair game for him. He talked some gal into getting into his patrol car and taking a drive one evening. They drove out on the lake road and were busy in the back seat when her husband found them.

"There was a scuffle and he grabbed Joe's gun. In the fracus the man shot Joe in a very embarrassing place. It could have been worse, for he was aiming at something else when Joe turned to run away. Let's say he won't be sitting down on the job for awhile. Now he tells everybody he was shot in the line of duty and is on sick leave. Shot in the line of duty, my foot! He was shot in his rump! Now he tells that he may get a medal!"

Darcy laughed. "George, that is his way of saving face! He probably made up that story in a hurry when he called his wife from the emergency room. Can't you enjoy the joke? It really is funny! Doubly funny because the man got away with atrocious behavior for years. Finally he got his just desserts."

"Yeah, you're right! It is funny! Except I have to put up with his stupid lies. And I have to find another deputy right away. I would like to charge the man with appropriating a patrol car for personal use! Wouldn't be worth it! Just cause more trouble!"

Darcy lowered the newspaper."Are you going to the rally?"
"Which one? I hear there are two."
"You're right! You have a choice! The dry's will meet at a local church with at least three ministers who will talk about the evils of drink. A man from the county crime unit will talk about the sale of liquor increasing our crime rate. Someone else will speak about an expected increase in divorce rate. Oh, yes! Minnie and Mo are scheduled to sing."
"That's a mistake! They should work for the other side. Their singing could drive any man to drink! What does the opposition plan?"
"The wets will meet in the local park. Since it's located on private property, they will serve free barbecue along with beer. They expect a large attendance. Very few people can resist free barbecue. The program includes a film about towns that already have free access to liquor. This is rebuttal of charges of increased crime and higher divorce rate. Their speaker explains a tax on liquor and how it will be used to improve our city hall, which needs a new central air unit. Also they have big plans to extend the town's water service and add new sewers. These are things we need badly."

Chapter Twelve

"Darcy, this is Aggie. Can you come over? George just called. He wouldn't tell me much, only that we will drive to the county seat to look at something. I have a bad feeling about this. I know in my heart he wants me to look at the girl they found. Would you mind going with me?"

"Of course not. I'll be right there."

"Ray, it was worse than a nightmare! Aggie was right. We went to identify a body. Good thing I went along. She was too upset to drive. As soon as we arrived, he told Aggie they were certain it was Faith but they needed her personal identification."

"I always wondered about that. Was it gruesome?"

"The county has no facilities for this, so the body was at the hospital, in the basement. Aggie went inside a room to look through a glass wall.

"It was Faith! She'd been in a creek for days! A dreadful experience for Aggie! Her beautiful daughter identified only by hair, clothes, and jewelry! Poor little cast-away doll!"

"Any plans for a funeral?"

"Not yet. They sent her to the state crime lab for autopsy. Could be two months before they release her. Poor Aggie! Her only child murdered ! No one to turn to! It's been weeks and isn't over yet! Once more she hangs in limbo!"

"Any idea how this happened?"

"Ray, they're not sure what happened, much less how it happened. They think she was shot!"

Rays chin dropped. "Shot! My lord, Darcy! I assumed all along it was an accident, a kid's prank that backfired! Who would shoot that pretty little thing? Like shooting a kitten!"

"She was shot at least once in the head and left face down in a creek under a bridge! The road is seldom used, in a remote area of large ranches. Because the ranches are large, very few people live there. It's heavily wooded, no mail service, no school bus route, an unpaved back road with an old narrow bridge. Ranchers pass through on their way to tend stock. In season, a few hunters drive through."

"Who found her?"

"A local rancher. He passes there every day but that day he happened to look down at the right time. Thinking someone lost a coat or a bundle of laundry, he walked down to the water. He could see a hand so he called the sheriff."

"Has anyone told Aggie that Faith was into drugs?"

"No. She won't believe it. George plans to wait for the report from the state lab. She'll have to accept that!"

"Does he have any lead at all?"

"Ray, he says very little but I'm convinced he does not. It's a bizarre crime with absolutely no clue. If you had to solve this crime, where would you start? It's hard to believe it of anyone in this town! Or one person that comes to mind! The local authorities are without a clue, stymied! They want the state crime bureau to handle it."

"Maybe George should put his energy into puzzles of why high school boys hang around at the "Y" every night. Does Marvin Grissom still run that place?"

"Yes, Marvin and Tina operate a quick-stop for gasoline, snacks, last-minute items. With hours seven AM to eight PM, takes both of them to handle it, but they are coining money! The boys show up after closing time."

"I agree with you. That is a puzzle. Why are they there? There is absolutely nothing there for them. I passed there last night. They seem to be waiting for something."

"They may have a long wait, Ray. Nothing ever happens around here!"

"You mean nothing happens except when innocent young girls disappear? Or sheriffs get shot with their own guns? How about our neighbor with her steady stream of afternoon callers?"

"Ray, when I go to church and see that woman playing the piano, I have to bite my tongue all through the service. Yet I cannot bring myself to tattle. Everybody despises a tattler. People will shoot the messenger. If I tell, the result is all on my head. I would have to live with that."

"You're right! It's none of our business! We must remember the problem may solve itself sooner without us. Most problems in marriage settle themselves if others stay out of it. Meddling should be listed as the eighth deadly sin."

"Once we were all friends. Our children played together! Nora may be ill, maybe with a brain tumor."

"Darcy, you're reaching for excuses! Bottom line, we stay out of it! We're too near them to get involved! They could patch things up and then both of them be mad at both of us for tattling. On a lighter note, I have another enigma for you. Our little neighbor, Trish Yandell, passes here early every morning. Has she taken a job?"

"That child? She's still in pigtails!"

"Have you seen Trish lately? A grown woman! Wasn't she a graduating senior this year?"

"You're right, of course! I simply lost track. I'll ask her mother if she's working. Could be a summer job to help with college expense. Her older sister attended college and I supposed Trish would, too."

With the meal finished, James and Gaylene left in other pursuits. Darcy spoke quietly.

Ray, I'm worried about Gaylene! That girl eats absolutely nothing!"

"Everybody eats something sometime or another."

"Haven't you noticed? She takes very little food on her plate. Then she plays with it! She toys with it until nobody pays attention, then hides in her room."

"Maybe she eats a big lunch at school."

"The cashier at the school cafeteria says Gaylene does not eat there. None of the teachers could tell me where she goes. She's so quiet, she can go anywhere she pleases and never be noticed. She's like a ghost."

"There's your answer. She uses her lunch money to grab a burger. Most teens could live on burgers and fries."

"I don't agree but it's something only a doctor can identify. Something's wrong with that girl and I know it!

"By the way, Ray, I asked Lola Yandell about Trish. She said Trish graduated in May with plans for college this fall. Then she got interested in the Fielding boy. Remember him? Nice-looking kid, lives several miles west of town."

"Do you mean she goes over to his house every day? That's odd! Did girls act like that when we were that age?"

"None that I knew personally. It didn't work then and it still doesn't work. Males always prefer to do the pursuing. Then I bumped into Laura Fielding yesterday and heard her version. Trish went over to their place early every morning, practically woke the people up. If his dad needed Ronnie's help with field work, Trish was always underfoot, wanting to be entertained. They were all growing weary of the routine.

"Then one night they sat down with Ronnie and discussed the problem. He's a kid with no experience at fending off aggressive young women. When his mother asked outright was he ready to get serious with the girl, he became very agitated and said he wasn't ready to get serious with any girl!

"The next morning Trish had a big surprise! When she arrived at the Fieldings for her regular wake up call, Laura Fielding stopped her at the door. She said Ronnie had enlisted in the navy, was already in boot camp. He is confined to quarters and not available for phone calls or letters until after basic training. She also said he had volunteered for sea duty and would ship out the day he finishes basic training."

"That boy joined the navy? Between supper and breakfast? On the sly? After hours? I didn't know you volunteered for anything until after basic training," Ray laughed.

"It has turned into a big mystery. Nobody knows where he is. He planned to attend Oklahoma University this fall. If I had to look for him, I'd start there. Wherever he is, he's still single and much wiser about women!"

"Thank goodness that's over! Local elections only serve to further divide a community! This liquor store question has done that! We already had enough petty differences."

"Now, Darcy, those old differences are always there. They stay buried until an issue is raised. Then they come swarming out again, like angry hornets and larger than ever."

"This fuss over a liquor store in town has brought up old scores better forgotten years ago. It always boils down to, "Nyah! Nyah! Your grandfather wet his pants in first grade!"

"I agree. Maybe we should let an impartial judge from another area make the decision and then abide by it."

"Now, Ray! That wouldn't work either! We could never agree on which judge to use. I'm sure the new liquor store will open right away. Does anyone know where it will be?"

"Jim Nance told me that nobody would sell or rent Main Street property to him. Too much stigma attached. So he bought a lot on the highway next door to Marv's. It is directly across the street from Lutie Wayman's house. She has an uninterrupted view of the back door and drive-in window. Swears she plans to rent seats on her front porch."

Chapter Thirteen

"Ray, I was right about Gaylene! We saw a pediatrician this afternoon. She does have an eating problem!"

"Did he tell you that all kids go through phases?"

"Ray, everybody knows about kids and their 'ages and stages.' This is different and I was right to worry about it! She may have anorexia."

"What in the world is that? Anything like acne?"

"No. That's skin. This is mental. The person feels fat, even though he's skin and bones. It can come over a person overnight. When it sets in, they stop eating."

"That sounds silly. People will eat when they get hungry."

"Not these people. They won't admit, even to themselves, that they are hungry. No matter how thin they get, they want to be even thinner. He made her strip to her underwear and weigh in front of him. She looks like a war orphan! Now I know she wouldn't go shopping with me because she doesn't want me to see how thin she is! She wears old baggy knit pullovers and baggy pants all the time, so it's hard to tell what she looks like. The doctor says it comes on with puberty. It's a subconscious wish to not grow up. They want to remain a child. He suggested counseling but says he has to find the right one. Not all psychiatrists can handle this problem."

A few days later Ray appeared at the kitchen door with a bundle concealed in his arms. He peered through the screen door cautiously before whispering hoarsely, "Where's Gaylene? I have something special for her!"

When Darcy returned with Gaylene, he continued his air of

mystery. "Come outside, girls. Gaylene. I have something to show you."

He bent to release a black and white bundle of fur that waddled over to sniff judiciously at Gaylene's sneaker.

"A puppy! A puppy! Oh, Ray, he's adorable! The prettiest puppy I ever saw!"

When she picked him up, he immediately licked her face. There followed a frenzy of playing, hugging, and laughing. She seated herself in the porch swing with him on her lap, singing and rocking him while he obligingly pretended to nap.

James, returning from his morning walk, was immediately drawn to the new pup. He seated himself in the swing beside Gaylene to pat its head and chuckle at the reaction.

"Hey, Gaylene, that's a fine dog! What's his name?"

"I haven't decided. We don't know him well enough to name him. We need to ponder on that."

"You're right! We should get acquainted with him first. I used to have a collie, looked exactly like this one. Best cow dog in the area! He'd cut out a calf and drive it anywhere I asked him to. When this one gets old enough to train, I can help you with that. Right now, we need to feed him so he feels at home. Puppies are always hungry 'cause they grow so fast. We'll find him a good place to sleep and make him a nice warm bed. Hey! I remember a dog house around here somewhere! I'll go hunt it up. We may need to paint it! Meanwhile, think of a really good name for him. A dog! This is great! I love dogs!"

Ray and Darcy retreated to the kitchen to allow the get-acquainted session plenty of room.

"Ray, that was a stroke of genius! How did you ever think of it? She's a different person with that puppy. This is the first time I have ever seen her really smile. Not that little pretend smirk she pastes on. A real smile and a very pretty one, too! I had no idea how pretty she is! By the way, this is the first time James and Gaylene have found a common bond."

"Just a happy accident. Clint Lassiter's collie had pups and it's time to wean them. The pups are purebred and would bring a good price but he just wants good homes for them."

Gaylene's smiling face appeared at the window. "I can love him and he can love me back! That makes us pals, buddies. I know! I'll call him Buddy!"

Chapter Fourteen

Darcy entered Marvin's Mini Mart to find Marvin and Tina behind the counter.

"I need my car filled with gas, Marvin. Tina, I need picnic supplies."

She puttered with choices as she chatted with Tina. "What are your hours?"

"We close at eight every night. We keep this place open thirteen hours, a long day."

"I don't see how you handle it. I know I couldn't. You must be especially well organized."

"It's just the two of us. We have our lunch delivered from Pearl's Diner every day. We share that, unless it's a busy day," Tina laughed.

"Darcy, I aired your tires and checked your oil," Marvin interrupted.

"Thanks, Marvin. By the way, I wonder about the boys who loiter here after hours? Are they a problem?"

"Darcy, I know about the boys hanging around here at night. So far, they haven't left even a gum wrapper. If people give their kids cars and allow them to stay out all night, it's not my problem. Until the boys do something I can complain about, I won't hurt my business by talking about it. I depend on repeat business. I can't afford to make folks mad at me."

Chapter Fifteen

She was a striking woman, tall, shapely. Enormous brown eyes were set in a perfect oval face framed by luxurious black hair. Her parents, astounded to have produced a classic beauty, gave her every advantage available to them. The town offered a limited selection of available suitors. The most eligible (translation: the one who could do the most for her) was a well-to-do rancher who upheld her parents' example and gave her everything she asked for.

Sylvia Vanault remained aloof from any part of ranch operation. Ranch wives wear jeans and plaid shirts and help out in critical times. Sylvia's designer frocks gave the impression she was on her way to tea. With jeans and boots the norm, she dressed to the nines and glided to the most comfortable spot in the room, content to be admired while adding little to the conversation.

The only person worthy of her total affection was her splendid son, Jeff. Born in her image, he was indeed splendid, tall, black curly hair, and those big soulful eyes. He, too, glided about, allowing his subjects to worship at the altar of his ego.

When Jeff turned sixteen, a new car completed his perfect image. With a set of wheels like that, it took only a few days to ally himself with Jeanette Allen, the prettiest girl in school. Jeanette, with peaches-and-cream skin, big blue eyes a man could swim in, a bushel of naturally curly blond hair you could wade barefoot in, could have posed for the cover of Teen magazine. Throw a cheerleader uniform on her and you had a girl every boy in school yearned for.

Not only were Jeff and Jeanette beautiful people, they were placed on the academic team. Now they were included in a tri-county scholastic meet. But Jeff, with his new status as car owner, scorned riding with the other kids. Why poke around on a crummy old bus with peons when he had the perfect car at his fingertips! He wanted to drive to the meeting.

His father objected, with all the paternal reasoning he could evoke. Jeff, an inexperienced kid, had driven only a few days on quiet by-ways near home but never in heavy traffic, never on freeways or strange places. Be smart! Be safe! Ride the bus! Leave the driving to us!

Sylvia intervened, for her perfect child was not to be denied. She would go along as the experienced licensed driver. Against all his better judgment and gut feeling but from sheer habit, the man relented. He had never denied her anything. He had no idea how to go about it.

As the kids arrived and boarded the school bus, Jeff and Sylvia glided along side. Like a shot, Jeanette left the bus to be seated beside Jeff. Walt, Jeff's best friend, appeared. Not waiting for invitation, he climbed into the back seat along with his latest girlfriend, Meg. Little Meg, fiery-red curls and big gray eyes, was giddy with excitement. She and Walt had been a couple only a few days and she deemed it a miracle to be included in this trip. She was all too aware that the first three were on the brain team while she struggled with her grades to play basketball.

Sylvia must have forgotten her promise to her husband to supervise the car trip. She suddenly extracted herself from the car to board the bus, announcing loudly, "I hadn't realized they turned this trip into a double date! I know when I'm in the way!" She looked about, smirking self-consciously about her handsome, popular son.

Right behind her came Billy Hollis, to quietly seat himself behind the bus driver, Greg Adams. Billy, star quarterback, was a good kid, not stuck-up or overbearing like some boys with all that prestige. The other kids liked him because he was nice to everybody. Teachers liked him because he behaved and made good grades. Billy wasn't brainy enough to be on the scholastic team so he hoped for a football scholarship.

As time for departure approached, the appointed sponsors entered the bus. Mrs. Dade, the typing teacher, dutifully went directly to the rear while Mr. Edwards, social studies, remained standing at the front, officiously counting heads and checking names on a list. Noticing Billy, he stiffened like a bird dog on point.

He barked, "Billy, why are you here? Your name is not on this list! Where is your permission note from your parents?"

Billy grinned sociably. "Aw, I'm along for the ride. I may attend the college you visit today. This way I can see if I like it."

"Billy, I cannot let you stay on this bus without a signed slip from your parents. If you're not on the list, you can't be here!"

"Aw, Coach! My parents work. I'll sit home alone all day. Can't I go along? I won't give you any trouble. I promise!"

"Nope! No Way! Things happen! I could be charged with negligence or kidnaping. If you had a note, I'd say yes! Billy, I'm sorry! I have to ask you to leave!"

The handsome, healthy boy left the bus to walk directly to Jeff's car. Opening the back door, he asked, "Room for one more?"

"Sure! Hop in!"

The bus wended its clumsy, bumbling way out of town. Turning onto the main highway, Greg, the driver, encountered heavy fog. It was like driving through heavy curtains to find yourself in swirling cotton fluff. His eyes widened, his face grew serious. Turning on all lights, he proceeded cautiously. After five groping miles, Jeff caught up with him. Greg hardly had time to note in his mirror the splendid car tailgating him when Jeff cut out, ripped past at high speed, to cut in short before roaring away into dense fog.

The soft murmur of the children's conversation ceased. They grew still, holding their collective breath, waiting. They knew. Five miles farther the bus filled with impressionable teenagers came upon a tragedy. Once more Jeff had passed in heavy fog. The perfect shiny car now lay twisted as one with a load of hogs.

A swinging flashlight was attached to a man in the middle of the highway. He told Greg to move the bus onto the shoulder and keep all passengers inside. Too dangerous to have people out in the fog. Greg complied and parked the bus in total silence. The awestruck, speechless children had ample time to take in the gruesome scene. The brilliant yellow car with black trim was unmistakable.

Sylvia glanced at her watch in annoyance, then flicked open her compact for a quick glance. She tapped her foot and looked about in boredom before her eyes drifted idly to the wreckage.

Reality struck!

"My boy! My boy!" She screamed as she leaped to her feet and began pounding on the door of the bus. "Let me out! Let me out, you fool! That's MY boy! He may be hurt!"

When Greg tried to explain, to restrain the woman, she cursed him as she wrenched open the door to race through swirling fog to the twisted wreckage.

Walter and Billy, on either side of the back seat, died instantly with broken necks. Meg, between them, ejected head first through the back window to die instantly as she hit the pavement. Covered with a raincoat, she lay like a broken doll. Jeanette, out cold with head wounds, was carefully placed in an ambulance, the bloody bundle recognizable by the fluff of blond hair. Jeff walked away without a scratch.

The trip to the contest was canceled, the prize was forfeited. The man driving the pickup was unharmed. His hogs were unscathed. His pickup was totaled. The bus load of teenage witnesses to the carnage had nightmares for weeks.

"Ray, I should feel honored. I made the first team! I was chosen for jury duty. What a day! They interviewed nearly every adult in town in effort to find twelve unbiased citizens."

"Wow! I'm impressed! How does it feel to rate with the unbiased?"

"I don't feel exalted. Not the least bit! A trial could last for weeks. I could sit there forever. After I was seated in the jury box, I got that closed-in pent-up feeling, like I was being incarcerated.

"Think, Ray! Everybody is mad at somebody! They want punishment meted out in large slices. That means I'm in the middle, damned if I do, damned if I don't. It's never easy to sit in judgement on your neighbor, someone you face every week the rest of your life!"

"Tell me again, who is suing whom?"

"The parents of Meg, Billy, and Walter sue Jeff's parents for wrongful death, for they enabled him to drive without supervision. The car is in the father's name, so he, in turn, sues their insurance company. These people want wads of money! No wonder the rates go up for all of us! The man whom Jeff collided with wants a new pickup and I don't blame him. He's entitled, another innocent victim."

"Darcy, people always ask for more than they expect. They know the insurance company will rate them lower than they ask, so they ask for incredibly large sums to compensate. It's a Catch-22 thing. You didn't mention Jeanette. What about Jeanette? Have you seen her since the accident?"

"Jeanette's parents ask for hospital bills, plastic surgeon's fees, cost of therapy and rehabilitation for her ankle, plus pain and suffering. She walks with a cane and may limp the rest of her life. Her ankle hurts with every step. She's lucky to be able to walk."

"Sounds like she's not so bad off."

"When compared to dead, you're right! Think about it, Ray! She was beautiful! One of those natural beauties who seem to glow! The kind that turns all heads. That's all gone! No scars, for she had a very good surgeon. Considering her face must have been hamburger the first time the man saw her, she does look good. She planned to enter beauty pageants all through college to pay for her education. Now that glowing beauty is gone. She is merely pretty, a kind of so-so pretty. The charming dimples are gone. Her smile is quirky, up at one corner, down at the other, giving her a lop-sided look. At least she doesn't frighten little children."

"I shouldn't ask. Have you formed an opinion?"

"Ray, a good juror never forms an opinion until he hears all the evidence. So maybe I am not a good juror. I have one opinion that I cannot admit in a court room. In my opinion Sylvia Vanault is guilty of something! She bailed out of that car in a fit of vanity!

"She was so proud of her handsome, attractive son, she let a load of kids drive off into a fog unsupervised! Gross negligence! As a result, three children dead! One is maimed! She should be punished! She should be locked up! What a grim turn of fate her child was unscathed!"

"Now the jury is chosen, when does the trial begin?"

"We were so engrossed in conversation, I forgot! After we were sworn and ready to start the trial, the man from the insurance company asked to settle. With a local jury and friends involved in the case, it would be hard to get an unbiased opinion. No telling what a sympathetic jury would award those parents. It will cost less to settle out of court. Now no neighbor has to decide against another neighbor. A blessing for the entire community!"

Chapter Sixteen

"Girlie, you've so been busy with jury duty, we haven't had time to talk. I keep thinking about that crooked banker! Like I said, I can eliminate the problem. Things should be planned. Planning is vital! Timing is important!"

"James, why do you think this is a solution?"

"Always worked for me! The first time I killed, I was in prison. This guy was mean! He carried a knife in his laced-up high-top shoe and everybody but the guards knew about it. Prison food isn't meant to make you want a return visit. You swallow it to keep from starving. The canteen was open a couple of hours per week and we looked forward to it. Though we were not allowed to have cash inside, I had an allowance on the canteen book. First time I got in line there, I got my order and turned away with a few candy bars in hand. That big, ugly thug eased up against me, stuck that knife in my side, and demanded it all. Second week, same routine.

"I never went back to the canteen. No use spending my bit of cash on that wide load of bad news. When I didn't show up, he came looking for me. He had the nerve to demand that I go to the canteen and buy things to give to him. When I told him I ran out of money, he didn't believe me. He threatened right then to kill me.

"Don't know what I would've done if the warden hadn't sent for me at that moment. When I walked into his office, my records were on his desk. He asked me to sit down and tell him about my life and my work experience. So I told him about my army career, my stint as a teacher, and my years on a working ranch.

"I never went back to my cell. Right then, he sent me to minimum security unit at Stringtown. That's a big ranch where they raise beef for the prisoners. Just think about it! In ten days, I am a 'trusty!' No high walls, no armed guards, no bunks chained to the wall!

"We slept in real beds in a bunkhouse and ate in the cook shack. We rode horses, worked cattle, built fence, just like at home. Each week, we butchered cattle for beef to send over to the prison. We kept a small stove in our butcher shop so we ate steak every day. It was hard work and long hours but I actually gained weight. It felt good to be outside on a horse, instead of sitting in a cell or cutting license plates.

"Just as I began to feel safe, here comes that big ugly dude with the bad attitude. He was all fired up to start our disagreement right away. I asked him to drop it. Let's forget it, I told him. I offered to shake hands with him. I laughed and said, 'No need to get testy over a few candy bars.' He still wanted to stick that knife in my gizzard. He was a gorilla, big enough and mean enough to do it, too!

"So I watched him! I watched every move he made! I knew he'd kill me if I ever got careless and I didn't aim to die over some candy!

"One morning we worked on the back side of the place. It was a dark day, cloudy, misty, trying to rain. We all wore big hats, jackets with collars turned up. Had to really watch our mounts. We were riding horseback and moving fast, driving steers to a pen in heavy trees and dense brush. I dismounted to tighten my saddle girth. While on the ground, I saw a piece of tree limb that made a good club. When I got back on my horse, I held that club 'tween my knee and the horse.

"I waited for a good chance and then I spooked a few steers. They ran behind a thick stand of trees where nobody could see us so I followed them in there. Sure enough, Old Bully Boy came crashing in right behind those steers.

"I saw my chance! I wheeled my horse around to come up behind him. I stood up in the stirrups to whack him on the back of his head with all my strength! He buckled and hit the ground like a sack of meal! Ha! The bigger they are, the harder they fall! When he hit the dirt, I landed right on top of him! When I was sure he was dead, I hid him under a big pile of dead brush.

"That night, when he didn't show up for supper, his name was added to the 'Escaped' list with no questions asked. Like I said, timing is all important. Add to that--the law in this town couldn't track an elephant in the snow!"

"James, I am impressed! You've led an interesting life! But that was a one-time fluke when you were younger and more active. You had strength because you feared for your life. It doesn't apply to this situation. Your state of health is of prime importance. Promise me that you will drop the subject."

"Like I said, that was only the first! Where I was in Alaska, you had to make your own law! Practice brings wisdom and expertise. An old head is a wise head."

Chapter Seventeen

"Hey, Freddie! Wait for me!"

"Move along, slow poke! I can't wait all night while you poke around like an old woman!"

"It's dark, Freddie! How do you see?"

"There's light from that sliver of moon. And from lights about the area. Shut your eyes for a minute. Then stand still while you open 'em just a slit. Your eyes will adjust."

"Okay. I can use a breather. Are you sure this will work?"

"Jim, why did you come along? You ask more questions than my kid brother."

"Who told you it would work?"

"Bennie Woods."

"Does he know for sure? Did he try it?"

"Shut up or go home! I thought you wanted a fix! Hey, Dave, you still with us?"

"Yeah, but you make too much noise! Be quiet or some night watch will hear us! Noise carries a long way on a night like this. Especially voices."

"Right! Here's the fence! I brought wire cutters! This should be a cinch. I need a fix! Let's go!"

Ray and Darcy slept soundly, the sleep of people who toil all day and welcome an early bedtime. The explosion rocked their house and shook them awake.

"Did I hear something?" Ray muttered. "I dreamed I was still fighting a war!"

"Ray, we both heard something! It shook this house like a chicken coop! Let's get up and look, to be sure it isn't us."

"While we look, turn on the TV. If it's anything important, there will be a bulletin."

In the hall, James bristled like an Irish terrier, wide awake, dark eyes snapping. Gaylene, pale and frightened, huddled near Darcy.

"Too brief for a tornado! Have we gotten into a war? That sounded exactly like shell fire!" James barked.

As they searched the premises, the nightly talk show on TV was interrupted. "We bring you this news bulletin! An explosion has just occurred one mile west of town at a storage facility belonging to a private oil company. Of the three teenage boys involved, one is dead, killed instantly in the explosion, and two are seriously burned, while fire rages in the storage area. Police and firefighters work to contain the situation. For a more detailed report, stay tuned to this station."

"Ray, from our front porch, I can see the fire! It's between us and town, near the storage unit that belongs to the oil company!"

At breakfast the next morning, they shared the morning paper while listening to TV reports.

"Here is an obituary for a senior boy in our highschool," Darcy noted sadly. "That tells us something."

Ray added. "Listen to this! Three teenage boys broke into a storage area to climb upon an oil storage tank. Someone told them they could get high by inhaling the fumes. They removed the large cap on top, causing the tank to explode. The nearest boy was killed instantly. The other two, barely escaping with their lives, remain in hospital with serious burns. The parents plan to sue the oil company."

"I have page three," James said. "Here is a statement from the oil company. They say they are not liable for damage or injury as signs are posted everywhere, on the gate, on the fence, and even the tank itself, stating, 'Danger! Not responsible for accidents'. There were 'No Trespassing' signs all over the place! They say they can sue the parents for damages to their property."

"Another dead teenager! Two more harmed, maybe for life! All because of drugs! Does it never stop?" Darcy moaned.

Chapter Eightteen

"Ray! I'm glad you are home! I expected you long ago!"

"It's a long story, Darcy. Sit down. On my way out of town, I passed Marv's service station. I was about to enter the highway when I heard a loud noise. So near, so loud, I thought I had a blow-out. At the same time I noticed the crowd of boys there were all running away, fast as they could go, in all directions, scattered like wild birds."

"Running away from you?"

"Of course not! At the same time, another boy came tearing out of the liquor store next door. He leaped out that door racing straight toward me, yelling his head off. Right behind him came Jim Nance. Jim had a gun in one hand and a baseball bat in the other, giving that kid a run for his money! It was something out of the Old West!"

"What did you do?"

"I stood still in the dark and waited. Darcy, you should have seen Jim! He was shot in the chest! Blood was streaming down his shirt! Yet he chased that boy and roared like a bull. He caught him by the shirt and shook him like a dog shakes a rat, even slapped him around a bit. Then he collapsed!"

"Is he alright?"

"He died, Darcy! His knees buckled and he keeled over to drop at my feet! I threw my arms around the boy and hung on while I yelled for help. In all the excitement, someone called George. He called an ambulance and they all came at the same time. Then I followed him to the station to make a statement."

"Jim?"

"Jim is dead! That fool kid went into the liquor store and pulled

71

a gun on Jim. He stuck that gun in Jim's face and demanded money. Jim laughed at him and said 'get lost'. While he was still laughing, the boy fired. George said he's on drugs and wanted money for more drugs. He was all shaky and nervous and scared. He said he never knew when he pulled the trigger, says the gun just went off! What a shame! I really liked Jim! This should not have happened!"

"Ray, does anyone know how our kids get drugs?"

"That's the real problem! Nobody knows. First Faith. Now this. How have we let drugs into this nice, clean little town?"

"We were all busy with our own affairs. We let it happen! Now we have a friend to bury, a nice little girl in the state morgue, another nice kid in jail for murder! Do we know this boy?"

"Do you remember Neil Watson?"

"Good heavens! Nice little boy in my first grade! Quick learner, high achiever. I thought he'd go to college and become manager of something. He's on drugs? Sticking up liquor stores?"

"George has him locked up without bail."

"This did not start with Faith Brandon! Drugs came first! I will pressure George to clean out the boys loitering there every night. If they hadn't been there, Jim would be alive. There's a connection between the boys loitering there and the drugs in this town!"

Chapter Nineteen

"I need a fill-up, Marvin. I'll step inside to speak to Tina."

"Darcy, it's just me. What you see is what you get," he laughed nervously.

"Is she ill? Out of town?"

"Neither. Tina left. She won't be back!"

"Marvin, I don't know what to say. 'I am sorry' is all I can manage."

"Don't waste your time being sorry for me! This should have happened long before now! I aim to tell folks so they won't have to whisper and pry to find out. Then we can get on with our lives. Tina and I could not agree on one big item. I wanted a family and she never did. At first she said, 'Let's get our own problems solved.' Then we started this business and she said 'Let's get the business up and running first.'

"Last time I pressed her, she admitted she never meant to have a family. She wanted money. She wanted things. She says kids are an inconvenience! Messy! In the way! I wrote her a check and she left with her car and her clothes. I'm single and I will stay single til I find someone who agrees with me about kids. Just think! We could have a couple in school by now!"

"You'll be a good father, Marvin. I admire you for knowing what you want and going for it."

Darcy found a morose George Moran at his desk. With her cheeriest smile, she placed a vase filled with flowers on his desk as she said, "These are fresh from my garden, George. This place could use a bright spot."

George's tired face broke into a smile as he leaned forward to bury his nose in the flowers."Mighty thoughtful of you, Darcy! Especially right now! Everybody in town is mad at me! They act like I shot Jim Vance! Sit down and let me cry on your shoulder. I feel plumb sorry for myself!"

"I didn't just drop by, George. I want to talk about drugs and crime here. Everybody in town is upset and you can't blame them. You and I both know something must be done about the drugs here or it will only get worse."

"Darcy, I've been busy about Faith Brandon and haven't given the drug problem enough attention. The state agents were supposed to step in but they're not doing much about it. They act like 'cause we are a small town, the case is not important."

He slammed his balled up fist into his other hand. "Doggonit! It's really got me riled up! It's MY town! Why can't I fix things!"

"George, it is my town, too. I'll say one thing before I leave. All the crimes committed here lately are linked to drug use. Find who is behind the drugs and the rest of it will become evident."

"Darcy, you're right, of course. I appreciate that you came to me with your ideas. Those old hens clucking over their back fences and their coffee cups chap my hide! They don't help anybody!"

"Ray, the authorities released Faith Brandon to her mother. The funeral is tomorrow. Aggie doesn't want a church service. She opted for grave side ceremony."

"Count me in. There will probably be a scant crowd. I can at least fill a chair."

Darcy shook her head. "You are wrong. Media publicity, notoriety, waiting, guessing, and local gossip, will bring out a record crowd, mostly curiosity seekers. Aggie doesn't want that. She hoped to narrow attendance to friends only. She needs friends."

"What about the father?"

"She finally tracked him down but he's remarried, has two little ones and another on the way. Says he can't scrape up plane fare and can't afford to take off work. According to her math, he had already started this second family when he left her. To put it nicely, they're not on best of terms.

"Then he had a lot to say about it was all Aggie's fault for letting Faith get on drugs. He said it's her mess so she can clean it up. He had nothing to say about how hard it is for a single mother to work full time and be mother and father at the same time. I'm certain he stayed away to avoid paying for the funeral. Funny thing—when some parents divorce, the kids get pushed aside, forgotten, left in limbo."

"How did Aggie react to the report that Faith was on drugs?"

"Better than we hoped for. She said it explained things she hadn't understood. She said if only Faith had talked to her, they could have worked it out."

"I have a suggestion. Instead of flowers, which are only a gesture, let's give Aggie a check. I am sure she can use it. Are the authorities any closer to finding the killer?"

"No. There isn't any place to start or anything they can get their teeth into. It may go 'Unsolved'. "

Chapter Twenty

Darcy breezed into the den to find Ray and James sharing TV baseball and a bowl of popcorn.

Excitedly she exclaimed, "Ray, remember the Cole family? There were three children and I had them all in first grade. Remember their father died when the second little boy was in my room?"

"Yes, I remember all of that. Tragic for a young man to die and leave a nice little family. Was it his heart?"

"Yes. Something there was no help for. The doctors could only tell him to not do strenuous exercise and not get excited. Useless advice. The man's heart was so fragile, he was in constant agitation. If the cat walked across the floor, he flew into a rage. That was hard for the children. They were too young to understand any of it."

"Now that you mention it, I do remember. Has something happened to the Coles?"

"The little girl, Nelda, the youngest, a sweet child but a problem. Always wound up too tight, constantly fidgeting. She wanted to be moving or hopping or running constantly. Not able to be still long enough to learn. I mis-diagnosed it as hyper-active. Immediately after she finished highschool, she married a local boy and has two very young children. The brothers grew up fine and strong but now Nelda has the same thing her father had, a heart-lung problem. She's twenty-three years old with same prognosis as her father– early death."

"How tragic! Can nothing can be done?"

"Medical science has made enormous strides with a heart-lung transplant, though it's loaded with risk and terribly expensive. The young husband is too naive to handle this situation so he left. Nelda, with no medical insurance and no money, is alone. She lives with her mother."

"You said expensive. How much?"

"A team of surgeons in Pittsburg do heart-lung transplants. She will be evaluated to see if she has strength to undergo surgery. If she passes muster, she will stay there until a matching donor is found, then undergo an eight-hour procedure. After surgery, she will stay for months to be sure the donor organ is not rejected."

"Sounds complicated and expensive! How much?"

"One hundred sixty-five thousand dollars."

"Wow! That is a bundle! Her family are wage earners with no prospect of that amount. Sounds hopeless!"

"Not so! Nelda had the preliminary tests and is able to make the trip. The entire community has gotten into it. The school is holding a carnival with all proceeds going into the Nelda fund. Children are out collecting cans and vowing to empty their piggy banks at the carnival. The Riders' Club has scheduled a rodeo. The Baptist Church plans a community garage sale while the Methodist Church is holding Bingo games with proceeds going to Nelda. The Drama Club is casting characters for a play. That sounds like fun so I pledged our help with that."

"Good Lord, Darcy! Have you signed me up to wear tight pants and a wig! I hate that stuff!"

"Now, Ray! Some people holler before they're hurt! This is team effort, charity, neighbor helping neighbor. The more people helping, the better chance for success. Don't overlook that it's fun to work with a play cast. If you don't want to act, you can be 'go-fer,' run errands and hunt for props. Or you can manage sale of advance tickets. More good news! The play is a Western comedy, easy for us. We can wear our own clothes."

"I can do any of that. If I can wear my own pants, I'll even be in the play cast. But only to help a sick little girl!" he qualified.

"Fine! James can be 'go-fer' How about it, Dad? With your experience in command and management, you are a natural. We can use all the help we can get."

James rose to the bait with his most gracious smile. "If it causes you to call me Dad, I'll be happy to do the job! I've never been a 'go-fer' but I'll bet even money I can get the job done. I should get out and mix, maybe run into a few old cronies, if they are not all dead," he laughed ruefully.

"We are having a bake sale tomorrow. One thing I can do is bake a cake. Where's Gaylene? I could use some help and Gaylene needs to come out of that room and re-join the human race!"

Darcy trotted to kitchen, calling out as she went, "Gaylene! I need you!"

Looking like an awakened owl, Gaylene came just inside the kitchen door to stand warily, as if poised for flight.

"Gaylene, you have your choice of jobs. Would you rather mix dough or prepare pans? I can handle three cakes. We can have three chocolate or we can mix it up. What do you think?"

A spark of interest began to glimmer in her eyes as she replied, "Can we have angel food?"

"Certainly! Good idea, Gaylene! Let's do angel food first so we can use the yolks in the chocolate. I have two angel cake pans. If I leave one cake here, would you eat it?"

"Um-Um! Yes, ma'am!"

"I want you to go along to help us with the bake sale."

"Yes, ma'am."

"While we are in town, we can look at clothes. How about that?"

"Yes, ma'am."

"I haven't paid attention to what kids wear now. What you would like to look at?"

"Everybody wears jeans to school. A few of them wear designer jeans."

Darcy's eyebrows flew up. "Designer jeans? To school? I may go into shock! I hear they're expensive!"

She began laughing. "This is funny! Kids began wearing jeans to school because they're inexpensive and durable. Now they wear designer jeans to school? Who ARE these people?"

"Well, actually only one. A senior boy. I used to like him but I don't anymore. He isn't nice like he was. I stay away from him."

"Does he have a name?"

"I hear he smokes pot. And does hard stuff."

"Gaylene, how do you know about hard stuff? Tell me about it. I really want to know!"

As she greased cake pans, Gaylene replied casually, "Oh, you know! You stuff it up your nose! Or shoot it in your arm! I don't know much about it but some kids do."

"They do this at school?"

"No! Of course not! But everybody talks about it when the teacher isn't around. Not very many people actually do it but they all know about it."

"And what is this boy's name?"

"We call him Max. I don't know his name."

Still absorbing this latest information, Darcy opened the oven door to check temperature. As an after thought, she spoke over her shoulder, "Gaylene, check the fridge. If we have an extra dozen eggs, I think I'll whomp up a couple of pies."

At that moment Ray entered the kitchen with a pair of pliers in one hand.

"Darcy, I tightened the brakes on your car."

"Um-hum. Thanks, Hon. Gaylene, how about those eggs?"

Ray, busy at the kitchen sink with a cool drink, looked around to see a strange creature on his back porch. It was covered with blobs of dripping chocolate icing, banana cream pie, and golden meringue. On closer inspection, it was dressed in Darcy's clothes.

"Darcy, what have you done!"

In a small, strained voice, "It's not what I have done! You knew I wasn't listening when you mentioned brakes!"

Gaylene came into the kitchen to stare and gape in stunned disbelief.

"Are you hurt?" Ray managed with a straight face.

"I'm not hurt! I am mad! I am hopping mad! A morning's work ruined! The car's a mess! Look at me!"

Wide-eyed innocence replied, "What happened?"

"With three cakes and four pies on the back seat of my car, I backed out of the garage and drove to the road. I barely touched the brakes. They grabbed, Ray! The car almost stood on its front end while baked goods sailed all around me. Some hit the windshield to barrage me from all sides! Some of them ricocheted all the way around to land in the back seat upside down! A chocolate cream pie hit me right between the shoulder blades!"

"I am sorry! What can I do!"

"We need a garbage pail, buckets of water, sponges and towels. When you have finished, bring my pans to the kitchen sink. I need a shower, shampoo and a change. Then I will start over on baking!"

"I'll take care of the car while you clean up." With a spark of mischief gleaming in his eyes, "But first I must have one kiss! In all my life I never had a chocolate cream kiss! Yum-yum-yum! Come here to me, you sweet thing!"

Ray cautiously leaned forward to claim his trophy as Darcy spoke.

"Honey, I'll stick with you!"

As their lips touched, they broke into giggles that quickly turned into guffaws. Gaylene stared in disbelief at two adults bent over howling with laughter. In disbelief, she rolled her eyes toward the ceiling before she, too, dissolved into laughter.

Wiping away tears of mirth, she said, "I'll help you, Ray. With one on either side of the car, it won't take long. I can help Darcy with baking and I can wash up. I have just discovered that I like to cook!"

Four people trooped through the kitchen door and into the den, to sit glumly in silence for a long moment.

"Darcy, whose idea was it to have this play?"

"I am sure it came from the Drama Club. Why do you ask?"

"It couldn't be a bigger mess! We should sell tickets to our rehearsals! More emotion is pored out behind scenes than on stage. When will What's-his-name let us work on our lines? He acts like we're doing a big time epic!"

MARTHA BAXLEY

"His name is Chester Phipps. He's a drama major and he coaches the annual highschool play. He wants it right and he wants us to get started right. We should all remember, he is exactly like us, a volunteer. We're lucky to have him."

"Maybe I'll get used to him. For a little guy, he sure can yell. If he pokes his finger into my chest one more time, I may deck him. But I hesitate to punch a guy who has to reach up to poke my chest. Oh, Lord! What am I going to do? How did I ever get into this!"

"His productions are a yearly event and a sellout. Let's don't lose sight of our original aim. We should make a bundle for Nelda. All projects are coining money and I have never seen this town so lively. The local baseball teams have scheduled a tournament for her. The newspaper gives free advertising space to all Nelda projects."

"Speaking of news, did you read about the daylight robbery east of town?"

"I haven't seen today's paper. What happened?"

"Someone robbed the older Mrs. Vanault."

"That nice little old lady! Who could be so mean?"

"Her house, on the main highway, is set back from the road with a tall hedge for boundary. Ideal, from a robber's viewpoint."

"What was taken?"

"Actually, not much. She answered the door to see a boy wearing a ski mask and hiding his hand in his pocket. He told her he had a gun and demanded cash."

"How much was taken?"

"She told him she never keeps cash on hand. Then he got angry and shoved past her so roughly that she fell and bumped her head against the floor. He stepped around her, found her purse, and rifled it. Only fifty dollars but it is armed robbery. She says she does not know her assailant."

"This is awful! She is a small lady. Is she alright?"

"She stayed overnight in the hospital. The report said she seems dazed but otherwise alright."

"We have more than our share of crime lately. George has his hands full!"

Four people trooped into the house, chatting and laughing.

"Great night! I enjoyed every minute!"

"I wouldn't have missed it!"

"Great performance! Glad to have a hand in it."

"Me, too! I'm tired, so goodnight!" said Gaylene.

"Ditto for me."James said as he left the room.

"Goodnight, Gaylene. Goodnight, Dad," Darcy said.

She turned to Ray, her face one big smile."Ray, I am so proud of you! You made the show!"

"I have to give Chester full credit. I finally figured out what a director is for. That little fellow got us to do things we wouldn't attempt on our own. By the way, you were great in your part. You should have gone into acting."

"I was cast as saloon keeper because of my red hair. They could call me Miss Kitty."

"The whole thing was terrific! The highschool girls with their bar room song and dance were delightful. When one girl kicked off her shoe and it sailed into the audience, they thought it part of the act."

"Gaylene actually ad libbed! She threw her garter out! I can't believe it!"

"It was a nice touch to put Minnie and Mo behind the stage to play and sing. Perfect background music."

"Let's face it. We were all great! But I want to know! Who knocked over that big stack of scenery back stage! Right in the middle of my big scene! I lost my train of thought and nearly flubbed my lines!"

Darcy laughed and hugged him as she teased,

"Ray, you are fishing for more compliments! After you've been lauded to the sky by the cast and everybody else! Okay! Now it's my turn! You were great as the father of the pretty girl! It was type casting but Chester knew what he was doing. You made the play worth watching! Clever of you, after that crash, to mention it sounded like thunder and we sure could use the rain."

"Enough! Any more and I'll have to buy a new hat! How much

did we take in? How much is in Nelda's fund?"

"Last time I asked, we have well over one hundred thousand. Can you believe that?"

"We're still short, even with our take on the play."

Darcy yawned as she murmured sleepily,"Ethel Mae Praether, at the bank, says an anonymous donor has pledged to make up the difference so Nelda can start her treatment right away. Oh, Ray! I just remembered! There's an antique safe in the bank. If we had known, we could have used it in our play!"

"Is our money kept in that thing?"

"Of course not, Silly! The real vault sits in a back room, big steel monster set on time-lock. This one is one hundred years old and definitely a novelty. The banker says it adds to the decor."

Ray shook his head in disbelief. "I never thought a bank needed decor. But times do change."

"It sits in out in the middle of the lobby, in plain sight, and isn't even locked, strictly for show. Compared to the real vault, the thing is a cracker box!"

Shaking his head, Ray muttered, "I'm still trying to figure out why a bank needs decor!" Reaching for her hand as he stifled a yawn,"Acting is hard work. I've had a long day. Let's go to bed!"

Next morning at the breakfast table, Darcy reminded them, "Today Nelda leaves for the airport! The whole town plans to turn out and wish her farewell. Are you coming? Ray? Dad?"

"Wouldn't miss it! Not after all the work we put into this! By the way, did anyone ever uncover the identity of the anonymous donor?"

"So far, nobody has a clue. We should leave early in order to park and find a good place to stand."

"Wow! I never saw a turnout like this! Not even when our football team went to the state final! I didn't know this many people lived in this town! Look, Ray! The school children stand in groups, holding banners. I'm sure Gaylene is with her group. Yes! Now I see her! Their banner says, 'We love you, Nelda.' And here comes the highschool band! Now I see her! I see Nelda! She's riding in Wiley

Reed's convertible, like a football queen! Isn't she pretty! I'm glad her mother is going with her. They are both crying. Isn't this sweet! I may cry, too!"

On the way home, Darcy was pensive for a long moment before offering,"I always wondered what it would take to pull this town together. I have never seen a public outpouring of love to equal this. I am sure a lot of it is because she is so young and pretty. Only twenty-two! But it is like a movie. It makes up for the gossip, silly squabbles, petty politics, and downright enmity between religious groups. We can all feel good about ourselves!"

Chapter Twenty-One

"Hello."

"Mrs. Parker? I am Mark Prince, the highschool principal. I am sorry to tell you that Gaylene is expelled from school. That makes her ineligible to ride the school bus and I cannot allow her to walk home. You will have to pick her up at my office before three o'clock."

"Gaylene is never a discipline problem. I would like to know what she has done."

"I'd rather talk to you in person. Meanwhile, she stays in my office until I release her into your custody. I expect to see you and Mr. Parker before last bell."

"What in the world has she done that I have to be dragged away from my haying and speed all the way to the school?" Ray groused. "Is she hurt? This makes no sense! If she is hurt, she should be in the emergency room!"

"Ray, I agree with you! What could I do? What could I say? I can't imagine mousey little Gaylene doing anything she shouldn't. Yet why should I be surprised! This whole town is acting crazy! Especially the kids! Maybe it's contagious! We must be grateful that she is able sit in the office for discipline. After seeing Faith Brandon on a slab, anything else a kid does is minor!"

"Come into my office and please be seated, Mr. and Mrs. Parker. Now, Gaylene, please tell your foster parents exactly what happened. Please start at the beginning."

Gaylene, pale and stricken, stared at her feet. Her mousey brown hair hung forward, hiding her face like curtains. She had been crying and was visibly fighting more tears. Gulping a couple of times, she gain courage to look at Ray and Darcy.

"I don't eat lunch in the school cafeteria. Since my parents died, I don't have an appetite. I try to eat but I do better away from large noisy crowds. I usually go to some place quiet and drink a soda."

Gaylene gulped noisily while she dredged up nerve to continue."Lately I've been friends with a new girl who just moved in. Doris Lee and I have a lot in common and we spend most of our time together. Today she was hungry and wanted more than a soda so we went farther.

"On the way back, we thought we might be late so we were walking fast when this car stopped beside us. It was a red Jaguar with two boys in it. One was Max. I didn't know the other. He doesn't go to school. Like I said, I don't like Max but Doris Lee does. She has a really big crush on him. They offered us a ride back to school. I would have said no, but right away Doris Lee said yes and hopped into the car, so I got in, too. I didn't know what else to do. After all, she's my friend and we were together. I know she likes Max and it was only six blocks to school. What could it hurt and we wouldn't be late."

As the tears welled up again, she looked about for a tissue. As Darcy offered one, she wiped tears before she continued.

"But when we got to the school, they didn't stop! We asked them to stop but they laughed and kept going. We drove out into the country and stopped on a little lane in a deserted area. They demanded sex, right then, right there!

"We were bawling and screaming at them to take us back! We said we would tell teachers, principal, parents, and the law! Doris Lee said she would go to the newspapers!

"Then the other boy got really mad and said he would hurt us if we told anybody! He acted mean! He said he had a knife! Then we were really bawling! That was when Max told him to bring us back and forget it.

"When we got back to school, the bell had rung and we were late for class. A teacher saw us get out of the car and sent us to the office for a hall pass. Nobody ever told me it was against the rule to ride in cars at noon! Max does it all the time and he gets away with it! How was I to know?"

All the way home Gaylene snubbed and snuffled and hiccupped while Darcy held her hand and patted her shoulder. As they entered the house, Gaylene mumbled about a headache and fled to her room. Ray and Darcy plodded into the den to collapse on easy chairs.

"Darcy, I told you this would not be a cakewalk! Now what do we do?"

"Poor little girl! Growing up is never easy for any of us, a nasty shock for some. Poor little Gaylene has never even had a car date, absolutely no experience with boys. She is a kid! Only fifteen! This could turn her against the male of the species forever! It's hard enough to grow up in a modern world, especially hard without your mother. I'll give her time to get her crying done in private before I talk to her."

"It was kind of Mr. Prince to re-instate her on the spot. First-offense plea! She really was a victim of circumstance. I am proud of her for having the spunk to mention that Max belonged there, too! I can only wonder why Max wasn't already there! Who is that mean dude in that red Jaguar? Why is he allowed to hang around the school at noon? He is bad news on wheels!"

"Gaylene, I know you miss your mother dreadfully, all the time. Times like this make you wish for her even more. I just lost my mother so I know exactly how you feel. I promise you that I will never try to replace your mother. Nobody can do that. But I would like to be more than Ma'am or Mrs. Parker. Can you call me Aunt Darcy?"

A timid little smile flickered. "I would like that!"

"Okay. Back to business. Did your mother ever talk to you about the man/woman business of sex and how babies happen?"

"Yes, of course. We got past that before I was ten."

"Did she ever talk to you about what to do if a man tries to force you to have sex?"

"Just a little. I've read about it and seen television shows that were explicit. But I never connected any of that to the boys I go to school with. They're just kids I have known forever."

"Honey, they can all be nice in public. You never know what kind of fellow he is until you find yourself alone with him. My grandmother once told me that she always wore a hat. She learned early on to use a hat pin if a guy got rough. My mother taught me about knees."

Through the tears, Gaylene smiled. "I know about knees. A family lived in our block, all boys but one little girl who was very pretty. Her brothers worried because she was so pretty, so they taught her the knee trick. One day when she was about fourteen, she was home alone when a neighbor man opened the door, walked in, and attempted to rape her. She didn't cry or panic. She simply waited for an opportunity to knee him in the groin. Then while he lay gasping for breath, she called the law."

"I never knew about that! Who was he?"

"Don't know. He was on parole so he went back to prison without trial. It wasn't in the paper."

"Honey, you made two big mistakes when you got into that car. First off, you say you do not like Max. When you feel that way about someone, it's best to stay away from them. Even though you don't know him well, your subconscious mind is telling you, he is not good for you. Second, you do not know the driver of that car. To let a stranger pick you up on the street is an unspoken agreement to have sex. You were very lucky to get away with it once. Don't ever do it again. You may not be so lucky another time! Be sure you know the boy. Give yourself time to get really acquainted with him. Stay with a group until you know him well enough to trust him."

"I feel so dumb to get in this mess! I wish I could move away tonight and never see these kids again!"

"Honey, you will feel foolish many times in your life. You can't run away just because you flubbed up. Learn from your mistakes. Above all, learn to laugh at them. When you feel foolish, don't run or hide from others. If you blush or cry or try to explain it away, they'll tease you and laugh until you really do want to move away. Learn to laugh at yourself. Be the first to laugh at your own mistakes and be the first to point it out to others. Say, 'Whoops! I made a mistake! Now what else is news?' If you laugh first, they laugh with you. You may find it makes you more likable."

Gaylene's face brightened as she sat up to swing her legs to the floor. "I feel better already!"

"Atta girl! Now let's find something cold to drink. Crying always makes me thirsty."

"Aunt Darcy, it makes me feel better to talk to you. I'll drink something and then I'll take Buddy for a walk. I haven't seen him all day."

"What about hauling those boys into court? I want them punished."

"So do I, Ray, but we can't do anything about it now."

"Darcy, they broke the law! They tried to force those girls!"

"Ray, the girls got into that car willingly! They were not kidnaped. A lawyer would cut them down in minutes. The boys never actually touched them. It's a shouting match. All they did was exchange harsh words and go back to school. Those boys will get caught soon enough.

"It's not in Gaylene's best interest to be dragged through a messy, pointless trial. It will create gossip and give her a bad name. Even worse, the other kids will remember it forever. Let it drop so she can get on with her life. She already has far more than her share of stress and grief. She also has an eating problem. Let's don't make that worse. I hope that doctor finds a specialist. She still eats very little."

Chapter Twenty-Two

Ray said, "Darcy, come out to the front porch with me. There is a beautiful moon I want to show you."

"Lovely! There is nothing I would like better than sharing a full moon with you!"

Hand in hand, they strolled out the door. Ray sat down in the porch swing and offered his hand to her.

"Let's sit here in the porch swing. Now come over here! Turn and lean on me so you can see what I see. Did you ever see anything so pretty!"

Leaning against Ray, she gazed dreamily at the sky. They sat cosily nestled a long moment, enjoying moonlight and quiet peace.

"Do I hear a mocking bird?" she murmured.

"Yes, the male sings all night while the female is nesting."

Darcy sat up straight. "Good lord! Now what do I hear? That cannot be any kind of a bird!"

"It sounds like voices."

"It's coming from the Lassiter house! They're screaming at each other!"

"I've been expecting this! It's long overdue."

"It's awful! I have never heard them go at one another like that! Let's move inside."

"Ray, it's been two days since that dreadful row we overheard at the Lassiter house. Today is Wednesday, the day the feed salesman stops there for an order. He usually stays about twenty minutes. Today he stayed at least two hours. Clint was plowing his back field, out of

93

sight of the house. It's so obvious what she is doing! I wonder how long before he finds out about this one?"

"All we can do is stay away. Whatever you do, don't ever mention this to anyone. We do not want to be involved."

"I was working in my front yard today when the man arrived there. I paid no attention because he stops every week. I worked until I grew tired before I noticed how long the man was there. I don't dare tell anybody what I see. I could be called to testify in court."

"Let's hope the situation never deteriorates to that! Surely she will run out of men to prey on. I'm sure she does this to even an imaginary score with Clint."

"Clint is a good, honorable man Any score she has with him is of her own making. All her childhood, her father spoiled her rotten. She gets her own way about everything or she never forgets, never forgives. She has turned this into a vendetta."

Chapter Twenty-Three

"Darcy, remember the old safe in the bank lobby? The antique for decor?

"Yes, of course. Why?"

"We had a bank robbery, right here in the middle of nowhere. Last night a couple of highschool boys stole a tow truck, hot-wired it, and drove to the bank. They broke out the front window with a crow bar and hooked the tow line to that old safe and hoisted it outside.

"The deputy heard the alarm and arrived to see the truck sitting crosswise in the middle of the street with the safe dangling mid-air. It's called getting caught with your hand in the cookie jar."

"Didn't anyone tell those boys the safe is an empty relic?"

"Sure they did! Right after they quit laughing! Now the kids are locked up for grand theft/auto and bank robbery. They were both high on drugs. George said they wanted money to support their habit. One of them is Jeff Vanault.

"Hang on! It gets worse! When questioned, he also confessed it he and a friend robbed his grandmother! When the sheriff spoke to the grandmother, she said it was indeed Jeff. She recognized Jeff's car. She could see a portion of it through a gap in the hedge. He sat in the car behind the hedge while his friend went to the door and pretended to have a gun."

"Another tragic mistake caused by drugs! We never had drugs in our town until recently! Faith was only the beginning! Now it's ruining one family after another! A connection runs though all these crimes! The obvious connection is drugs! Why can't the law see the pattern?"

"Can you see a pattern, Darcy? Don't ask others to do something you can't do."

"Two things stick in my mind! Anything out of character bothers me, anything counter to the norm. The most obvious is that crummy camper sitting in that nice residential area in town. It showed up about the time this drug and crime wave began. Why doesn't it bother anyone but me?"

"Is anyone living in it?"

"Nobody knows. It showed up there and nobody knows anything about it. It looks deserted. But it should not be there! That part of town is not zoned for campers!"

"Darcy, if the people living there don't complain, what can we do?"

"We can ask questions!"

"Who would you ask? Nobody ever comes near it!"

"I'll work from a different angle. That lot has been vacant since the Murphy house burned years ago. Mrs. Murphy lived alone and after her home burned, she moved away rather than rebuild. It could have been sold a dozen times since then."

As Darcy approached City Hall, someone call her name. She turned to see a young couple with a small child.

"Mrs. Parker! Remember me? Carla Simpson?"

"Carla! Of course I remember you! One of my favorite pupils!"

"Oh, Mrs. Parker, all of us were your favorites! We caught on to that years ago."

"You're right! I loved all my students. Now you must introduce me to this young man."

"This is Simon Hix, my husband, and I'm Carla Hix now. This is Lacey, our little girl. She's two. And there will be another in about three months."

As Darcy turned to acknowledge the introduction, she was struck by the young man's slack-jawed, vacant stare, the restlessness, inattention and odd, slouching posture.

Carla rushed to explain. "Mrs. Parker, Simon worked in a large plant in Tulsa and it paid well. We bought a house and had a baby. Then one day at work a large crane ran amok with the big hook swinging from a cable. The hook hit Simon on the back of his head. They rushed him to the hospital and he was unconscious for days. The doctors said he wouldn't live after a head injury like that. Then they said that was a miracle he lived but he'll never be any better than he is now. After he was released from the hospital, I brought him home. We live with my parents now and his mother lives here, too. They all help me care for Simon."

At a loss for words, Darcy looked at the young woman little more than a girl, yet burdened with an extra-wide load of responsibility. Impulsively she reached out and patted her shoulder.

"Carla, I want you to know if you need anything, you have only to ask."

"I take care of him best I can, Mrs. Parker. I do the very best I can. I don't know how long I can go on, with two little ones."

Darcy impulsively hugged the girl as they parted.

"Ray, it took my breath away to see that poor man! He's young, healthy, attractive, with a strong, athletic body. But he's drastically brain-damaged with no chance of getting better. His eyes are totally blank. He has no memory except he does respond to the sound of her voice. She has to watch him constantly and it's obvious they are both miserable. I wish we could do something for them."

"Darcy, it's sweet of you to want to, but must you mother the entire world?"

"You have only to see Carla and you would feel the same way! She is a good little mother to their child. She sincerely wants to care for him, too, but it's too much for one person. I know there is something we can do!"

"Did you learn anything at the hall of records?"

"Yes, I did! And I was right! That is the old Murphy place! After the house burned, Ada Murphey moved away. She went to live with a daughter in Lawton and died not long ago. I have the daughter's name and mailing address. That was all I could ferret out."

"You have viable information. Now what do you plan to do with it?"

"The records are open to the public but I have no authority to pry into other people's affairs. I will think about it. There's always a simple way if you approach a problem logically."

"It sure is nice of you to ask us out to your place, Mrs. Parker. It's been a long while since we went anywhere except to a city park."

"Carla, the pleasure is ours! We have plenty of room at our place and we have run out of kids, not counting Gaylene. Here we are! Lacey, would you like to see our chickens?"

"She's never seen chickens. She may be afraid of them. Simon, take my hand. Let's all go this way. Lacey, hold my other hand."

"Mrs. Parker, it's lovely at your place. It was good to spend the afternoon in the country. Simon enjoyed playing with your puppy as much as Lacey did. He could walk about the pasture and look at everything to his heart's content. When we go to a park, people act afraid of Simon so I keep him near me. I don't want anything to cause him to be sent away!"

"Carla, do you mind if I stop for gas? I forgot that on my way in."

As she guided the car to stop near the gas pumps, she spoke to the young man who hastened to serve her.

"Hello, Marvin. I need gas. I'm sure you remember Carla. And this is her husband, Simon Hix. And this is Lacey. She's two."

"Darcy, what do you think you are doing?"

"Ray, I gave an exhausted, over-burdened, expectant young mother the afternoon off. We sat in the porch swing and kept an eye on everybody and let her have a few hours rest. That poor man walked about, looking at everything and enjoying his freedom. In town she has to watch him closely, for his sake and the sake of others. Out here we can allow him more leeway. He is impulsive but not violent. He saw flowers, birds, animals. He especially liked Buddy. I plan to have them out once or twice a week until the new baby comes. That poor girl has good intentions but there's a limit to what one person can do!"

"Ray, I asked Carla and Simon out for the morning. They should be here in a few minutes. Any suggestions?"

"We are getting ready for pecan harvest. Is he capable of gathering pecans? I use machinery for most of the work but some trees are hard to reach. That means I'll have to ford the creek with my equipment. Would be simpler to do those by hand if I could find someone willing to work."

"Ray, that was a wonderful idea! He liked it so much, he stayed out there all morning. Well, to be honest, we all worked. We made a game of it and even little Lacey got into the spirit. We had to coax him to come in to eat lunch. The weather is lovely and it's a pleasure to be out in the woods right now. We had a foliage tour all the way there and all the way back. It was like a picnic. Simon is happy when he can use his hands."

"I have several trees he can harvest. I'll reserve them for his visits. If that poor creature has found anything he can do, then so be it."

"The pecans are all harvested. Wonder what we can find to keep him busy? He can do simple jobs. He likes using his hands but he can't be left for more than five minutes. He can't remember very long. When he forgets, he can get into trouble. To make it even worse, he has absolutely no reasoning power. I don't know how Carla will cope after the new baby arrives."

"Who was on the phone?"

"That was Carla! She has bad news! She wanted to tell me that Simon woke in the night, moaning and holding his head. They took him to the hospital and he died early this morning, massive brain hemorrhage, a direct result of the accident. Doctor said it was a miracle it didn't happen sooner."

"Darcy, it's hard to grieve for someone as damaged as Simon. He got very little pleasure from his limited way of life. Maybe this is better for all concerned. Poor Carla couldn't handle two babies and him, too. She did not want to institutionalize him. She stayed in mental anguish."

"I know all of that. I grieve for the person he was before the accident. The accident that never should have happened."

"At least he had a few peaceful hours here. I'm glad you found a way to help them."

"Hello."

"Mrs. Parker, I want you to know my baby is here and he is fine. A little boy. I hope he looks like Simon."

"I am glad for you, Carla. When may I visit?"

"We came home this morning. You can come by any time."

"I can't wait. I will be along in about an hour."

"I need gas, Marvin. Is anyone inside?"

"I'll help you as soon as I finish here. I can't find decent help. Would you be interested in helping me out a few hours per day?"

"Why, thank you for thinking of me, Marvin! Let me think about it."

"Marvin, I don't want to work full time but I know someone who does. Carla Simpson just had her baby and as soon as she's able, she wants to work a short shift. Her mother plans to baby sit for her. That girl has been through a nightmare! She needs out of the house and back into the adult world. Something that keeps her busy and in contact with other people is indicated."

"Hey! I hadn't thought of asking Carla! She's okay! Really alright! I admire that girl mightily. I saw how she took care of Simon. Not many men claim the loyalty and love that man had. She's a fine person! I'll call her tonight. Thanks, Darcy! I'm in your debt!"

Chapter Twenty-Four

"Darcy, our attorney called while you were out. The hearing about your deed has been placed on the docket for next spring."

"You were right! You said it may take years. Why does it takes so long?"

"The county holds court for a certain number of days, usually two or three weeks in the spring and again in the fall. They summon jurors and hear as many cases they can while in session."

"Didn't you get a summons for jury duty once?"

"Yes, I did. And I served, though I left my own business unattended."

"Why didn't you explain that to the judge and let someone else take your place?"

"Even though it was an inconvenience, I felt the accused deserved a jury of his peers, which means equals. If I were accused of a crime, I'd rather have somebody like me on the jury than somebody who was there because he had nothing else to do."

"I understand, but please don't say that in public. Some folks might think you're bragging."

"It certainly is not bragging! I work hard and I pay our bills. Our property tax is always paid on time! The tax list and voters list is used to draw names for jury duty. I felt it was an honor to serve!"

"Why does it take so long to bring a case to court?"

When a case is presented to the court, it's placed on the docket in the order it is filed. Some cases take longer to hear than others, so they never know how many they can clear off the docket. Sometimes long-winded lawyers chew up everybody's time. If they run out of time, they carry your case over to another session."

"No wonder it takes forever! But I can wait. I have to live with the outcome even though I may not like it!"

Chapter Twenty-Five

"Hello."

"Darcy, this is Ethel Mae Praether at the bank. Have you heard about LouAnne Rawls? She's very ill! There is a serious problem."

"I didn't know! LouAnne and I were in school about the same time. She was LouAnne Reed back then. She married Clyde Rawls, didn't she? I haven't seen much of them lately. I thought they moved away."

"They moved back here about a year ago. Their only child, a little girl, is about four years old. The reason I called, LouAnne is ill with cancer. They have no insurance and no savings. They are at absolute standstill for medical help until someone steps in. The community did so well with the drive for Nelda Cole, I thought there might be a chance to help these people. I was impressed with your diligence and energy in that. We need a coordinator for the drive and I thought of you."

"Ethel Mae, I'm flattered that you ask but that's a terrific undertaking! I need to think about it."

"Please don't take too long! That girl needs help right away!"

Darcy replaced the phone and turned to Ray. While explaining the task to him, her eyes filled with tears. She stopped mid-sentence and left the room. She returned shortly, eyes still wet but her face was calm.

"I can't help thinking about that little girl losing her mother! I miss my mother every day but I'm old enough to be grateful for the long, full life she led. I watch Gaylene struggle with her loss each day. Something must be done to help these people and we have no

103

time to lose! I'll call Ethel Mae right now and tell her I will do it! I have some ideas for getting started. We have to get at it!"

The next day at lunch, Ray asked, "How's the drive for LouAnne coming along?"

Counting on her fingers, she listed, "All the local churches responded with bake sales, raffles, or just plain passing the hat. There is a pot on the counter at the bank with a sign that says, 'Pitch in for LouAnne Rawls.' The American Legion has scheduled a benefit dance with all proceeds going to LouAnne. That's the best we can do on short notice."

"Sounds like you're off to a good start. Here's my check."

"Thanks, Ray. We thought to collect as much as we can right away and present it to them. This should get them started with doctors, treatment, and hospital costs. We can continue to work on it as they will need money later. I hope to come up with better ideas as we go along."

Darcy dropped into her chair in the den and swept off her hat. She wiped her forehead and fanned herself with the hat. "Ray, while I was in town, I noticed one of those traveling religious groups has come to town. They set up a large tent on the vacant lot next to the hardware store. They papered the town with big, garish, gaudy signs, handouts, flyers, whatever."

"They'll stay a couple of weeks. When interest wanes, they'll move on."

"And good riddance! We have churches of all faiths right here, available all the time. I don't understand why people give credence to these things. It can lead to disaster, like Jim Jones and the Guyana tragedy. Remember that mass suicide?"

"People are drawn in by curiosity or boredom. Or they go there because something is lacking in their life. When there is a need in a person's life, he is apt to drift from one thing to another."

"You make it sound like only the dissatisfied or emotionally disturbed people would be interested."

"There's more to it than that! Some of those men are real spell-binders. There are people who enjoy listening to them."

"I personally disapprove on general principal! It drains money away from our town, money that our own churches need badly. Money that's invariably funneled into an individual's pocket. But, hey! Sounds like you are interested! Do you plan to attend?"

"I don't think so. Though it could be enlightening to see who, and how many, of our neighbors show up."

"That's morbid curiosity! For a few minutes you held me spellbound with your religious philosophy. These things were popular a century ago, when people attended because they lacked entertainment and enlightenment. In this day and age, I am astounded to find they still survive."

"They will always survive for those who can cast a spell. I thought most of them moved into television. I remember the story of old Billy Sunday, an evangelist of earlier days. Someone asked him point blank if he thought getting religion ever did anybody any good. He answered that he thought getting religion was was like taking a bath. It couldn't hurt anything and it could do a world of good."

"I brought a flyer that might prove interesting. It lists a Reverend Mr. Orel Algood as leader of this merry band."

"Orel Algood! I am shocked! Are you sure about that name?"

"I'm sure I read well enough to read that. Why?"

"I remember something! Wasn't there a man living here at one time, a man named Orel Algood? He ran a used car business! I am positive I remember the name! It always struck me as especially funny for a used car dealer! I had a good laugh every time I drove past there. Many used cars can be all bad but his slogan was 'See all good cars at Algood's Car Lot."

When James wanted his daughter's company, he automatically headed for the kitchen. He found her busily preparing their evening meal.

"Darcy, have you seen Gaylene?"

"She took Buddy for a walk, Dad. Why do you ask?"

"I want to teach her to drive. Fifteen is old enough for a learner's permit. I need something to do and I'm a good teacher. With your permission, I'll work with her a few hours each week."

"A wonderful idea! I'm glad you thought of it! Here she is now! Gaylene, come hear what James has to offer!"

"We're back!"

"How did it go? The first driving lesson? Any squeakers?"

"Aunt Darcy, it was fun! James let me drive his car and it was great! I can hardly wait til I can have my license! I can hardly wait til I tell the other kids! And when is supper? Anything I can do to help? I'm starved!"

After their meal, Darcy and Gaylene were finishing the dishes when Galene casually mentioned, "Aunt Darcy, there was an announcement at school today. There is an opening on the cheerleader squad. Trials will be in two weeks. I want to try for it!"

Darcy stared open-mouthed for a brief moment before she recovered enough to answer, "I think that's a fine idea, Gaylene. Have you ever done anything like this before?"

"No, but my mother did. I meant to do so last year but the accident changed all that. I couldn't because I was too upset and didn't feel like cheering. Now I feel better and I want to do it!"

Cautiously, Darcy offered a feeler. "Are you sure about this? Two weeks is not a long time to train. You will need a crash course. Who do you know well enough to come over after school and coach you?"

Gaylene became dramatic. With clasped hands, she pled, "Aunt Darcy, I am positive! Oh, I know! I'll ask Doris Lee! She was a cheerleader in junior high in another school. We both want to try. There is room on the squad. Besides losing Faith, two girls are graduating. Wouldn't it be the greatest if we both won!"

"Sure, Hon! Bring her with you after school. We'll drive her home after practice. We'll do all we can to help you."

At bedtime, Darcy spoke to Ray. "Ray, Gaylene wants to try for cheerleader. I am worried! That wouldn't be so bad but trials are only two weeks away! That doesn't give her enough time to prepare.

Even worse, she has no experience, no background, nothing to prepare for this! It boggles the mind to imagine mousey little Gaylene as a cheer leader! The things kids dream up!"

"We have to support her! Remember how we always encouraged our kids to try new things!"

"Yes, we did, in spades! But I'd feel better if she had more time to prepare."

For days, Gaylene and Doris Lee bounced and bounded about the back yard after school. The entire place echoed the cheers emanating from them. After days of determined routine, Gaylene knew all the yells and she had the gestures right. Yet from the kitchen window, Darcy watched and listened. And wrung her hands in despair.

When Ray came to the house for a cool drink, Darcy drew him near the kitchen window as she murmured,

"Watch this! Something is just not right! She does all the yells and gestures okay. But, Ray, she is awful! Watch her feet! From the waist down, she's a dead stick! She'll never win like this! Watch her routine and tell me what is wrong with her feet!"

After a moment of peeking from the window, Ray grinned as he gave Darcy a quick, one-arm hug. "You're right! Her feet don't work with the rest of her. I can fix this! Just watch an old soldier in action!"

He strolled out to the back yard to stand about, as he watched the girls. After a moment, he interrupted.

"Girls, would you like a bit of advice? When I was in the army, I drilled every day. I remember it very well. When you want to turn, do thus and so. Now watch my feet," he commanded.

Ray executed a perfect turn. As he did so, he said, "That's called a pivot turn. It is quick and neat and it gets you there every time. Now watch it in slow motion. You place your toe thus, then turn your body as you place the other foot. Perfect one-eighty turn! Now let me see you do it."

"Hey, that's neat! Thanks, Ray! You make it easy!"

He patiently watched each girl pivot. When they had the hang of it, he rejoined his wife in peeking from the kitchen window. Standing behind her, he could easily peer over her head. He hugged her close to him contentedly as he buried his chin in her hair and murmured into her ear, "Now, madame! I present to you, two whirling dervishes! Anything else I can do to restore peace in our valley?"

The day of the trials, Darcy joined the spectators for the trials. Poor little Gaylene, alone in the world, needed someone rooting for her. And in all honesty, she could not bear to wait until school was out to know the outcome. But, she promised herself, she would not hover! No need to make the girl nervous.

"I feel like I'm on trial," she thought. "I hope she places and above all, I hope she doesn't place last. Let her be spared all of that."

She watched each contestant carefully, with her own mental tally of how she would rate the girl if she were a judge. When it was Gaylene's turn, Darcy held her breath through all the turns, moves, gestures, and chants. When each girl had her turn, the judges retired for conference, Another cliff-hanger! Finally, the judges appeared and Doris Lee was named first. Then Gaylene's name was called and as she took her place with the squad, Darcy waved at her as she breathed a deep sigh of relief.

At bedtime, she said, "Ray, I couldn't have been more concerned if I were a contestant today! Gaylene has been hurt enough by the loss of her parents. It wouldn't be fair if she lost this. I know it's not the same but these issues are important to teens. A loss would be a disaster when she is just recovering from grief."

Ray wrapped his arms around his wife.

"Honey, you're sweet to fret about her, but it turned out okay. Now you have one more job--cheerleader mom! I know you remember sponsoring the girls on away-from-home games, late nights, last minute emergencies. How about the night Jennie lost her pom poms? How can a girl perform without them! What a squeaker! Lucky break you remembered she left them in the trunk of a parent's car."

Ray looked up as Darcy sank into her chair. She kicked off her shoes and fanned herself as she spoke.

"Rushing about in this heat! Whew! We collected all our donations and had a grand time counting it. Then we took it over to the Rawls' house. It wasn't as much as we hoped for but still enough to get them into a good oncology program. They face surgery, hospitalization, chemotherapy, and long recovery. We gave them a cashier's check for ten thousand dollars. We hope we can come up with more later."

"Sounds great! By the way, something bothers me. I have been thinking. And remembering. Did Clyde Rawls have a drinking problem?"

"He did when he was younger. I remember his last year in highschool, he did gain a reputation for drinking. I thought he quit all that when he grew up. I haven't heard about his having a drinking problem since they returned. Come to think of it, we never heard much about them after they moved away."

At that moment, Clyde Rawls held the check with both hands. He moved nearer the light to look at it again. He hadn't meant to, hadn't planned it, but after Luanne went off to take a nap, he took the check out of her purse. He only meant to look at it, in awe of the loving generosity of the people of his little home town. Sure, he and LuAnne both grew up here but they had been gone a few years and people tend to forget.

But when they moved back, it was like they had never left. Her father helped him land a job right away and a good thing, too. He was flat broke. He hated when that happened.

He knew LuAnne was not herself since their return but if he thought about it, he supposed she was still ticked off at him. Lord knows she had plenty of reason, because of the scrape that had cost him his job. He never meant that to happen. LuAnne quietly pointed out–he never meant any of those things to happen, but when he was drinking, things always happened. Even after he promised to stop drinking, she was never the same.

When she finally told him she was sick, he thought it was something simple, routine, maybe another baby. It was not a good time for that to happen! He pounded his fist into his other hand in frustration. He had stayed around the house too much after he got fired from his job! Another of his messes!

He would always remember the moment when he heard the diagnosis. He remembered how he felt the pit of his stomach drop down to his knees. In shock, he could only think in partial sentences. Not LuAnne! Not the big C! That only happened to old people! People who were ready to die anyway! Not his LuAnne!

He hoped it wasn't brought on by something he had done! He had put his darling through years of stress and vexation because of his drinking. He knew it hurt her something terrible to lose their house. In his clumsy way of an apology he told her, you can always get another house! If you are lucky, that is. But THIS!

When those people brought that check and laid it before them, her big brown eyes lit up and she looked more like the girl he dated and married. She sat up straighter, pushed her curly brown hair back from her tired face, and smiled like the old days.

He pushed his thick mop of unruly dark curls away from his ruddy face and licked his lips. Pale blue eyes gazed at the ceiling as he tried to remember how long since he had a drink. A year! An entire year! Lordy-lordy! How he needed a drink! Just one drink! Just one!

He had promised to stay sober and he had stayed sober! Until now. All that money! Surely it wouldn't make any difference if he had one little drink! Just to celebrate the fact that help was at hand. He licked his lips again. Just one little drink to help him feel a little better. By George! He deserved one drink! Having a sick wife was no day at the beach!

"Ray, Ethel Mae Praether just phoned. There has been a tragic turn of events. Clyde Rawls took that check we gave them. He waited until LuAnn was asleep, took it from her purse, cashed it, and went on a big drinking spree. When he was too drunk to have any reason left in him, he wandered into the traveling revival tent. He went in and sat down while they were singing. Someone handed him a songbook and he joined right in the singing, roaring and bellowing out at the top of his lungs.

"When the preacher made the altar call, Clyde Rawls leaped up to stagger to the altar. Then he fell down on his knees right then and there! He cried! He prayed! He bawled and begged for forgiveness! Then he asked the preacher to pray for LuAnne's recovery. After the prayer, Clyde gave every bit of that money to him! He had his pockets stuffed with large bills and he foisted it off right there! Did you ever hear of anything so tragic?

"Sheriff Moran has Clyde locked up for public drunk. He found him at daybreak, under the town water tower, sitting in his car with the motor running, sleeping it off. Oh, yes! The revival show moved on during the night, right after the meeting ended."

Ray reached for his hat as he strode purposefully to the door, saying, "I'll go into town and talk to a few of the men. There may be something can be done about this."

Ray looked at the clock as he entered his home. "Whew! It has been a long, hard day!" he told Darcy dejectedly. Shaking his head, he reported, "Darcy, George went with us. We located the traveling show a few miles east of town. The Preacher Algood has disappeared and the others don't know, or won't tell, where he is. George put out an all points bulletin for him but I doubt it does any good. If they ever find him, he won't have the money on him. It wasn't robbery and it wasn't coercion. There were too many witnesses to the scene to dispute there was."

"Isn't the fact that Clyde was drunk a factor in this? Hasn't anybody ever heard of diminished capacity? Too drunk to know what he was doing!"

"It wasn't coercion and Clyde didn't sign anything. Neither did the preacher. It was unethical for the preacher to take his money when the man was obviously drunk. But you will have to find the preacher before you can extract justice. Even if you can find the man, you will never find the money. The money will disappear mysteriously. Even if Clyde sued and got a court judgement against the preacher, he will never got the money back!"

"Darcy, it seems to me that LuAnne knew his problem. She could have made another provision. She, of all the people in the world, knows exactly how weak he is. Yet she left that money right under his nose when she went off to take a nap! If she didn't feel like going to the bank to put that check in safe keeping, she could have called her father to come take care of it. She could ask the committee to do that errand for her. She must have a death wish to set Clyde up like she did."

"Ray, you sound cold and heartless but I completely understand. I'm so disgusted with this fiasco, I'm resigning as chairman of the drive. I have run out ideas on how to hold out my hand and ask people for their hard-earned money."

Chapter Twenty-Six

"I just heard on the radio in my truck, there has been a jail break. Jeff Vanault was out on work detail. He was with a crew on the highway picking up trash near a used car lot. A man pulled off the road along-side the car lot and stopped a few feet from Jeff. He got out to look at a car and left his keys in his pickup. That was all Jeff needed. He did a quick flit, jumped into the pickup and took off. Did you ever hear of anything so dumb! There's an all points bulletin out on him."

"Did they give a description of the truck?"

"Black Dodge, late model, gun rack across back window. Good ole boy type," Ray replied. "Keep the doors locked. Better safe than sorry."

"He's probably across the state line, miles away by now. As I remember, Jeff likes to move fast."

The boy pressed himself close to the house, all the while listening. He was positive that he hadn't heard a sound for several minutes. Inching nearer the back steps, he squatted behind a large azalea bush. At that moment the back screen opened to let Ray out. The boy remained frozen behind the shrub while Ray descended the back steps, walked quickly to the barn whistling all the way, climbed onto his tractor and roared away toward his field.

The boy cautiously stood. After a careful scan, he quietly climbed the back steps, crossed the large back porch and quietly opened the screen door. Seeing nobody inside, he quickly stepped into the tidy, inviting kitchen. Though the kitchen was spotless, it was evident that food had been prepared recently. The kitchen range was still warm and he could smell something tantalizing, like savory meat and juicy pie. He was hungry but above all, he was thirsty. He opened the refrigerator to espy a tall pitcher of lemonade. Prompted by intense thirst, he grabbed it with both hands to quickly drank big noisy gulps from the side of the pitcher. Thus engaged, he did not hear Darcy quietly enter from the hall.

"Hello, Jeff."

He straightened and whirled to face his former teacher. White-faced, trembling, he blurted, "H-hello, Mrs. Parker."

As to an invited guest, she politely asked, "May I help you find something? You must be thirsty! Would you like something to drink?"

"Yes, ma'am. Anything wet would be great. I really would like a big glass of cold water. I'm dry as powder."

"Here's a glass of water. Are you hungry? I have cookies. Or you can have something more substantial. We just finished lunch and there was a nice piece of chicken left. It's still warm."

Jeff sat down at the kitchen table. For a full minute he tried to muster defiance and bravado. Failing that, he lowered his head onto folded arms and burst into tears. Sobbing like a six-year-old, he wailed, "Oh, Mrs. Parker! I'm hungry! Thirsty! Hot! Sweaty! I'm homesick! Tired! I was never so tired in my life! I walked miles through thick brush and tall itchy grass! Through briars! Mesquite! Mud! Prickly pear! I have done nothing but walk since early this morning. I thought I was really slick when I saw my chance and stole that truck. I was sure I would be miles away before they could get out an APB. Would you believe it only had a little bit of gas? It ran dry before I got around the corner! I left the truck, climbed over a fence, and walked along the creek that runs across your place. Now I'm in more trouble than ever!"

"Jeff, sit down. You should cool off before you eat. While we wait, let's talk about your choices."

"Choices?"

"Sure! We all make choices every day. You made a bad choice when you robbed your own grandmother. You made an even lousier choice when you drove away in that truck this morning. You were charged with grand theft/auto plus bank robbery. Today you have added a charge of escape plus another charge of grand theft/auto. Now I want to know, is your next choice to hit me on the head and steal my car? Is my husband coming home to a smiling wife and a decent supper or will he walk in to find me battered and needing the emergency room?"

Jeff began sobbing again. "Oh, Mrs. Parker! We all love you too much to ever hurt you! I was stupid to think I could make a break! I wish I never even tried! How do I ever put it all back together!"

Her heart ached at sight of the sobbing boy. Stop it! Enough! She admonished herself. He's had enough of that silly mollycoddling! She calmly pulled out a chair to seat herself across the table from him. At eye level, she spoke quietly but firmly.

"You can't undo any of that! But you can decide to never do anything as stupid as that again. You're the only person who can decide what you do. You can decide to grow up and take responsibility for your actions. Does that make sense?"

Wiping sweat and tears from his face, he replied, "Makes sense to me! I wish I hadn't got myself into this mess! I'll go back farther than that. I wish I had never smoked that first joint!"

"That's another choice. Remember, hindsight is always twenty-twenty. Maybe I can help you. But first, you can help me. Jeff, you were always a good boy and a good student. I want to know exactly what happened. I want to know about the first joint you smoked, the first hard stuff, and I want to know exactly where you got it. While I fix you something to eat, tell me about some of your choices. I promise I am absolutely shock-proof! I want to hear all of it! Every last detail!"

Jeff wiped his eyes and blew his nose. He drank long and slowly from the glass of cold water before him. Then he took a deep breath.

"Mrs. Parker, I don't like being in jail! I never gave it much thought until I was locked up! Like an animal in a cage! In jail, you're no better than an animal! You can't eat or drink or sleep or even use the bathroom in privacy! I'm an animal on a leash! I would give anything if I could go back to being a good kid with a decent future!"

"I'll make a deal with you, Jeff. Finish your lunch. Then you

need a shower and a nap. When you have rested a bit, I want you to
tell all this to Sheriff Moran."

"Is he going to be mad at me?"

"Jeff, that is the silliest question you could ask! Right now,
everybody in town is mad at you! You have brains! You have a strong,
healthy body! You have good parents, decent, hard working people
who can give you a decent education! You don't appreciate any of
that! You threw it all away with both hands! You won't do anything
useful or productive! You prefer bad company and bad hours! You
think it's cute to misbehave while the other kids gawk at you. You
only want to get into scrapes! Each of your silly scrapes is worse
than the last!

"You need to think about your choices. You can choose to behave
and be a productive citizen or you can sit in a cage. Do you want to
spend the rest of your life in a cage? Or will you choose to cooperate
with Sheriff Moran?"

"Mrs. Parker, if I could go back to where I was before I smoked
that first joint, I will do anything you say!"

"Jeff, I believe you mean that. Now start talking! I want to hear it
all. Start at the beginning and don't leave out anything!"

"George, This is Darcy Parker. I have wonderful news for you! I
know how you can apprehend Jeff Vanault, single-handed, and solve
some other problems at the same time. When can you see me?"

"That sounds like another fairy tale. I'll be waiting in my office."

"I will be waiting at my place. More privacy here. We don't need
an audience."

"Jeff, Sheriff Moran is on his way here. Before he gets here, you
must understand what you will agree to. First, you must agree that
you will cooperate completely with the sheriff. You will tell him
everything you know about drug operations in this town. You will
name names and you will agree to tell the judge the same thing.
Because these are adult decisions, we must first call your parents
and your attorney before there is a formal agreement. Are you willing

to do all of that?"

"Yes, ma'am! I've had enough of being dumb. I will do anything you say!"

At George's knock, Darcy cautiously opened the door and looked around before she stepped aside. She led the way into the den where Jeff was waiting.

"Sheriff, I'm sure you know Jeff Vanault."

"Jeff and I are well acquainted, I'm sorry to say! Jeff, what can you say that won't further incriminate you?"

"Sir, I have talked with Mrs. Parker and she has some good ideas."

"Darcy, what's he talking about?"

"George, you know all about how Jeff is in bad trouble, facing a sentence that could be years. He will become a hardened criminal with a long record, lost and useless to society, unless we can turn it around. He has a way to help you if we can work it out. He's willing to help but we must call his parents and his attorney before we do anything binding. Before we call them, I think we should discuss it privately. The fewer who know, the better for Jeff."

"Jeff, she's right, of course. Let's see if we can work a deal favorable to both of us. I'm in just about much trouble as you are!"

"Mrs. Parker said I should begin at the beginning. Okay! Right after that bad wreck when I killed three of my friends and ruined my girlfriend's face, I tried drinking. I know I'm only sixteen but we can get booze anytime we want! It's not far to the state line and some of those Texas joints sell it out the back door to minors with no questions asked. Then one night we were all standing around at Marv's, half-smashed, when someone offered me a joint. I never smoked one but I knew what it was. I had enough liquor under my belt to think it was a good idea.

"After I smoked it, I never felt better in my life! It was like flying! I could go to sleep without seeing all those dead and butchered faces. So I went there every night, just to buy the stuff. Everybody says pot is no worse than tobacco. Just 'cause it's illegal is no reason to deny yourself. Some laws are bad and should be removed. Everybody says that!"

"Jeff, that is not what everybody says. That is what pot smokers say to justify their action. But let's stick to the facts. I want to hear all of it."

"After I smoked pot for awhile, one night I was high when someone asked if I would try something better. I was already flying high! Why not get higher? Oooh, it was great! Until I came down! Then I needed a fix and I needed it bad. That's when we robbed Gramma. I'll always feel bad about that. She was never anything but goodness and love to us. I really love her. It never would have happened if I hadn't been on something! I want to get clean enough to make it up to her."

"Jeff, do you know who brings this stuff into our town? Who is dealing? Who sells it to minors? I want to know! I don't want any maybe-I-do, maybe-I-don't stuff! I want the truth!"

"I don't know the supplier but I know who sells it to the other boys."

"Are you ever going to tell me?"

Darcy intercepted. "George, he knows enough to steer you in the right direction. He is known to the crowd of boys who are into this. He knows one or two names. He does not know the supplier.

"This is his deal. He works with your department and helps you solve the drug case. That earns him a chance to prove himself. You and I both know there is no point in putting a minor in prison to come out ruined and useless. I know exactly what hardened prisoners do to younger ones, especially one who looks like Jeff. It makes me sick to think about it! There is no point in doing that to a silly, misguided underage kid when we can get rehabilitation for him right here! Jeff, I want you to tell George what you can do."

"Sir, I will help you with the drugs if you will help me with the drugs. I will lead you to the dealer if you will find a way to get me into a detox unit. I don't care how long I have to stay there! Anything is better than prison! I will stay there until I can come out drug-free! Then I will go to college. I promise! And I will never, no, never break the law! It just is not smart! If I can do all of that, I want the charges against me dropped. Most of all, I don't want a prison record to follow me the rest of my life."

"Jeff, I can live with that. Now let's call your parents and your attorney! Then we must talk to the judge. We have work to do!"

Chapter Twenty-Seven

"Ray, I'm going to Lawton for the day. James will keep me company. I may not be here when Gaylene comes home, so I hope you will be. I don't like to leave a young girl alone, especially as isolated as we are."

"I'll do better than that. We'll have a driving lesson. She can drive the truck while we take Buddy to the vet for his booster shots. Happy shopping!"

As they drove away, James and Darcy exchanged conspiring looks.

"This should be right up your alley, Dad. You like intrigue and walking softly. I don't like to leave Ray out of things but he'd have a fit if he knew. Beat on his chest and swing on a grapevine like King Kong, to shield me from danger when there is no danger. We will ask questions. That's not endangering ourselves."

"Right, Daughter! Keeps my blood circulating and my mind sharp. With a one-hour drive, we have time to get our stories straight. Exactly what do we plan?"

"I'm searching for information about a woman who lived in our town for a number of years. Her house burned one night. Burned to the ground and left her with nothing. Her husband had died and she had no incentive to rebuild. She went to live with her daughter in Lawton. Her property has been vacant for years. I want to know if it's been sold, and to whom."

"Why do you care? Why does it concern you?"

"That property is a scant half-mile from the trailer park where Aggie lives. It was vacant property until about the time Faith disappeared. Now a shabby camper trailer has appeared there mysteriously, incongruous, conspicuous in a nice neighborhood. Anything out of sync bothers me. Nobody knows anything about it, making it into a mystery. Is it left there by some camping enthusiast who wants free parking space? Is someone living there secretly? Or is it abandoned? With all this crime wave, Faith murdered, many of our children on drugs and out at night committing crimes, I want to know if there is a connection. I like to tie up loose ends."

"Sounds reasonable. How do you plan to do this?"

"First stop, the newspaper. We want to look for Mrs. Murphy's obituary, to name all the family members. The records at City Hall were sketchy. Sometimes people don't leave their property to the most obvious heir. I have known of people leaving their estate to their cat. We merely want to identify all of the players."

"Well, Girlie, we searched the obit column. Now that you know all the family names, where do we go from here?"

"We don't know much more than we did. In addition to the daughter, Adelia Murphy Henderson, there was a grandson. I have an idea! The daughter still lives here. I have her address from tax records. Let's pay a visit to the daughter. Mrs. Murphy was about your age. Now it's your turn to be sleuth. You may lead the conversation."

He patted her on the shoulder as he grinned roguishly. "I'll do better than that. Watch me in action!"

They found the house in an older part of town. On well-cared-for lawns, houses marched down the street like well-scrubbed but threadbare old soldiers standing at attention. When James rang the bell, the door opened and he found himself facing a tall, bony woman with narrow piercing eyes.

"How do you do? I am James Shannon. I'm looking for an old friend of mine, Ada Murphy."

The woman squinted suspiciously at James. After a long, scathing stare, she asked, "Why do you want to see her? Are you a summons server?"

With his most charming smile, James assured her, "Ada and I were close friends when we were young. Then we grew apart and each of us married someone else. I've been away for many years. Now I'm looking up old friends and classmates. Just want to talk about the good old days,"

"Did she owe you money?"

"No way! I'm planning a meeting, a reunion of old classmates. I'm merely trying to contact as many of my school chums as possible to see if my idea is feasible."

Again, James used the big, warm smile, the gracious, courtly manner. His white western hat in one hand, he almost bowed over her bony hand.

The woman still squinted suspiciously at the handsome older man. His smile, coupled with merry black eyes and an air of expectancy, quickly thawed some of the suspicion. The frozen face warmed slightly and her voice was almost cordial.

"A-ah, would you like to come in?"

"Just a moment! Let me introduce you to my lovely daughter. Darcy, we have an invitation to go in. Will you join us?"

At sight of Darcy, warmth drained from the woman and suspicion returned. Barely audible, she opined, "Humph! Daughter, my foot! Old fool!"

Through introductions, James made comments of, "Nice of you to ask us in. It's a long drive and we both need a break. My, what a lovely home you have!"

They entered the house in time to see a young man exiting hastily. They saw only his back as he moved rapidly along the hall and out of sight. Pretending not to notice, James continued his commentary.

"Been a long time since I spoke to Ada. Wonder if she remembers me?"

They seated themselves to see the woman narrow her eyes to a squint. She spoke forcefully. "Tell me again! Tell me in words of one syllable! Why do you want to see my mother? She moved away from there years ago. You're the first people from back home to come looking for her."

"I have more than one reason to see Ada. We want to ask if her property there is for sale."

"Ha! I thought I could smell more than old friends!"

Triumphantly, the woman folded her arms, leaned back in her chair to smirk derisively.

"My mother died last year! She left everything she had to me! That's my property now and I'm in no hurry to sell! The longer I keep it, the more it's worth!" she boasted.

After an awkward silence, Darcy spoke. "It's getting late. We should start home soon, Dad."

"Right, Daughter."

Outside the house, Darcy took a road map out of her purse and took her time to unfold it and spread it upon the hood of her car. She motioned James to join her in examining it. Poring over the map with their heads together, Darcy spoke softly.

"Dad, is that a red Jaguar I see in her garage? The garage door is at half-mast but if you look closely, you can see one fender and the rear end."

"Aha! Yes! Yes, it is! If there's a lick of sense between us, we'll head for the old corral! We have already seen too much! Come on, Girlie, let's move out!"

As they drove away, Darcy asked, "Well, Dad, just what did we accomplish?"

"We identified the current owner of the vacant property. From the obituary, we established that Ada Murphy had one grandson. Probably the young man we glimpsed, the one who did not want to see or be seen by us! We know a connection exists between a young man in that house and the goings-on in our town. The red Jaguar is the key. Not many of them in these little country towns. That thing sticks out like a sore toe!"

"Let's keep this information to ourselves. It doesn't prove helpful unless we can tie it to our problems at home. Let's think about it, at least overnight."

"Right! Remember my motto, 'Breathe through thy nose!'" James chuckled gleefully as he slapped his leg.

Chapter Twenty-Eight

Replacing the receiver, Darcy turned to Ray.

"That was Carla Hix. She and Marvin have decided to be married. She wants us at the ceremony."

"Isn't that a little fast? Did they ever touch second base?"

"They have more in common than many couples I know. They are young, handsome, healthy, intelligent individuals. They are hard-working and ambitious. They have known one another all their lives. Their families get along well. They even belong to the same church. When they were in school, Marvin was older and got interested in girls before Carla was old enough to date. Now the age difference only makes him more interesting to her. He has a thriving business and a lovely home. All of that aside, both their first marriages ended tragically. Another factor they share is overwhelming loneliness. Sometimes when you meet the right one, it's like coming home after a long trip. It must be like that for them. Oh, I must tell you! They want us to stand up with them! They insist."

It began as a chuckle that quickly grew to a crescendo of roaring laughter. Gaining control of himself, he wiped his eyes and grinned knowingly as he spoke, "Well, of course! This is just recompense! Let no good deed go unpunished! All matchmakers should know beforehand they shall be forced to join the wedding party!"

"Ray! You know it did not start out that way! It just happened! I had no way of foreseeing Simon's passing!"

"I've been meaning to have a little talk with you about that very thing. Where do you keep your crystal ball hidden?" Ray teased. He dodged and exited laughing as his wife threw a sofa pillow at him.

They were met by a smiling, breathless Carla, a far cry from the wretched girl who brought her disabled mate home to die. Today she wore a festive pale pink dress and her face was glowing. She threw her arms around Darcy.

"Mrs. Parker, Mr. Parker, I'm glad you could join us today!"

Marvin, tanned face glowing, hugged Darcy as he extended his hand to Ray.

"Same for me, too, Darcy! Ray! I have never been so happy in all my life! I can hardly believe my good luck! I'm getting a sweet little wife and two of the liveliest kids I could hope for. I have a good start on that family I always wanted."

"We are happy for both of you."

"Darcy, it is not 'both of us.' All four of us are getting married. It couldn't have worked out better if I planned it. I wanted kids. Now I have two and we plan a couple more, at least. I hope they're all as pretty as my wife!"

Chapter Twenty-Nine

Returning from the wedding, they entered their home to hear the phone ringing.

"Hello, Baby Sister! Anything happening in good old Dullville?"

"Why, yes! We just got home from a wedding for two special friends of ours. James is teaching Gaylene to drive. Gaylene is also learning to cook and that can get exciting. Especially when she burns something. Wish you could be here! I could talk for days about all the things that happened lately."

"You may get your wish. How about next week? I suddenly have 'use or lose time' I'm bound to use. Can you fit me into you busy schedule? How about Gussie? "

"I love it! This couldn't happen at a better time! Will you call Gussie and talk to her? Make her feel included. I haven't seen her since Mama's funeral. I thought to give her plenty of room for pouting and then let her make the first move. This visit is just the occasion to give her a reason to leave it in the past and move on."

"Right! See you next week!"

"Ray, Anne's plane arrives at Wichita Falls at 6 PM. We should be on our way to pick her up."

"Darcy, there's no way I can go. I have a sick cow and the vet should be along soon. I would ask James to go along but I need his help til the vet gets here. Can you handle this?"

"Of course! Anne and I can have a good gabfest on the way back, catch up with girl talk. It's a one hour trip and I just have time. Give me a kiss and I'll be on my way!"

Darcy left her drive, turned into the county road, and in a few minutes entered the highway traveling west. Moving along at road speed, she suddenly became painfully aware of a large black cloud looming on the horizon. As she moved directly toward it, it grew more menacing by the mile.

I hate to be a baby but that thing really bothers me! I should have checked the weather channel! The weather has been so pleasant, I never gave a thought to turbulence. If I were not a big girl, I'd turn tail, drive straight home and crawl under my bed. But Anne's expecting me! This will probably prove to be a little rain squall that makes me laugh at my own fears. In this country, one never knows what the weather will do next.

The rest of the trip was spent with one eye on the road and the other on the weather. By the time she reached the airport, the entire sky was an ominous black. Lightning played from cloud to ground and from cloud to cloud. She parked and raced into the terminal to find Anne waiting. Her sister got a hasty greeting sandwiched between news about the nasty turn of weather.

A breathless Darcy advised, "We should go straight home and stay there til this blows over."

"Suits me! I grew up here so I understand completely. I remember how folks tease about it. They said, if you don't like our weather, wait a few minutes and it will change. I have no desire to tangle with a monster tornado! Let's go!"

As if to validate dire prophesies, they left the airport and entered the eastbound highway in time to feel the brunt of the storm as it hit. Visibility was limited to a few feet in front of the car. It was like driving though a wall of water. The rain fell so hard and fast, the highway looked a stream.

"Thank goodness there's not a lot of traffic! The storm is enough to contend with!" Darcy said. "Tell me about your flight. Tell me about your job. Do you still play golf?"

So Anne talked, Darcy drove, the storm raged, and the rain poured.

At last they reached the crossroad where Darcy turned off the highway onto the county road leading to her house. At the last curve before reaching her house a stream was crossed by an ancient bridge.

"It's the old creek bridge. Remember this?"

"Lord, yes! We used to fish here! On hot afternoons, we sat on the bridge and dangled our feet over the side. It seemed cooler that way."

Darcy stopped the car to stare at the crossing.

"What is the problem?"queried Anne.

"I can see water. That tells me the creek is out of bank. I want to look at it up close before I cross that bridge. I'll leave the head lights on while I take a look. Wait here."

"I have a better suggestion. Let's both look at the stream. Two heads are always better than one."

The sisters left the car to walk onto the old bridge. The angry stream was indeed out of bank and approaching flood stage. The inky surface was visible only where highlighted by the car beams. Water flowed a scant few inches beneath the bridge understructure. Under their feet, they felt the old bridge quivering in protest against the force of the rising stream.

"Well, Darcy, what do you think? Is it okay?"

"Yes, for the moment. The water is still rising. In another few minutes it may be over the bridge floor. Let's not waste time!"

They returned to the car. Darcy crossed the shaking bridge and at last, to the house. The next morning the bridge was under water.

"Good thing we came home when we did! Otherwise we would be lolling around in a motel with breakfast brought on a tray while these guys fend for themselves," Darcy teased Ray as he returned from assessing the storm's aftermath.

"How much rain did we get last night, Ray? I am betting it was a bunch."

"Darcy, our rain gage ran over but the weather man on TV said we got sixteen inches."

Anne said, "I remember something else Mama used to say. She liked to tease visiting strangers. She would tell them our average rainfall is sixteen inches and last year it all came on a Tuesday."

"Darcy, dinner was delicious! Real home cooking! Now it's time for you sit down with the rest of us. Come sit by me." In invitation, Anne patted the sofa cushion beside her until Darcy complied. "Gussie, you must sit by my other side, as we used to do."

Augusta stood stiffly for a moment before she relented to seat herself beside Anne at the other end of the sofa, as far apart as possible, and sniffed. Smiling, Anne placed an arm around each of her sisters and drew them nearer.

"We should have pictures now. First, the three of us together. Then all of us with Daddy."

After Ray snapped enough photos to satisfy everyone, Anne spoke.

"We have waited long enough, Daddy! We have to know! We have wondered all our lives, what became of you? You never wrote or tried to see us. What were we to think?"

"Like I told Darcy, the day I left to serve time at the state prison at McAlester, Sara told me to never come back. I knew it would be hard to never see you three again so I went as far away as I could go. I decided to go so far away I would not be tempted to sneak back for a quick glimpse. I went to Alaska.

"At first I moved about, sizing up everything as I went. Back then it was still all wilderness. Right away I found a job in a gold mine as bookkeeper. Soon after I arrived, there was a big change in management and I was asked to work in the mine as supervisor. I had been an officer in the army so with my experience with leading men, it worked out fine. It paid much better than office work. My wages were fantastic but it was isolated, miles from the nearest crossroad. I made good money but there was no place to spend it. I stayed as long as I could stand it before I quit and moved into town.

"At first I worked in a casino as faro dealer. Then one day the boss decided to go south and offered to sell the place to me. He took all the money I could rake up and trusted me for the rest. I made good wages in the gold mine but that place was better than a gold mine! It coined money! I paid for it in three years. I had friends and a fine life style, but I finally grew tired of all that. All I could think of was Sara. I wanted to see her one more time. I wanted one good long look at her before I die."

He dropped his chin onto his chest as one tear rolled down his cheek. Darcy patted him on the shoulder and gave him a quick one-arm hug. Gussie sniffed and gathered her things for departure as Anne broke the uncomfortable silence.

"Come on, Baby Sister, let's walk Gussie to her car. Gussie, tell me a good time to drop by your place for a good gabfest. I have only a few days vacation and I want to make the most of it."

Strolling along, they chatted casually but when they reached her car, Augusta stood a long moment, fidgeting with her keys. For the first time that day, she looked into Darcy's eyes.

"Darcy, I meant to call you. I really meant to, but things have been a mess at my place. I didn't call because I haven't felt like talking. Jon, Ellen's husband, has moved out. He has been my son-in-law for twenty years, so I'm in shock We are all in shock."

"Gussie, I am sorry for the grief and turmoil. Does anyone know what is their problem?"

"Oh, yes! It's not their problem! It's his problem and we all know what it is! He decided he is gay!"

"That suck-egg hound! After all these years! After two kids! Aren't both their kids in college? " Anne declared.

Darcy spoke, "This is a disaster! What about Ellen? How does she handle this?"

"Ellen has surprised us all. They've been together since high school, so we were sure she would fall apart. No way! She took an aloof approach. First, she moved their joint accounts into her name only. This was strictly a precaution, before he had time to do something really foolish. She says she will take extra courses at the college and try for a better paying job. Beside two kids in college, they have a big house payment. She needs a larger income to hold things together. She has an attorney to help her and she plans to charge Jon with desertion. She will not grovel or beg, or even discuss terms."

Gussie wrung her hands. "I don't know what anyone can do until

Jon comes to his senses! I try not to say anything. Sometimes couples split up and then reconcile. I don't want to take sides and then wish I hadn't. Surely I couldn't be blamed for taking Ellen's side? I don't know what to do! I pray a lot."

Anne chimed in, "I remember when they were dating. They couldn't keep their hands off each other! There was no question in his mind about his sexuality then. I was relieved when they eloped. At least they made it legal. Now, after all this time, he thinks he is gay? What came over the man?"

Gussie's lip quivered. "I think it's all the news we hear about gay rights and gay bars and gay bashing. I think he is curious. It may be a new kind of mid-life crisis."

"Could be his way of getting attention. He was always a control freak. He can't stand not being the main attraction. I think Ellen is right. We should all of us take the hard-hearted approach. Ignore it. Perhaps it will go away," Darcy advised.

Mournfully shaking her head, Gussie chided, "Now that is exactly what I am trying not to do, Darcy! You are taking sides. And you, too, Anne. I will pray for both of you."

Darcy looked into Gussie's eyes and spoke. "If there is anything we can do, you have only to ask. Otherwise, it's hands-off for us! The less said about this the better. Like you say, sometimes they split and then go back together. The fewer who know, the better for all. Idle gossip is never good for any marriage. I won't breathe a word to anyone."

"Anne, I have errands in town and I'm sure we will see a few of your old friends. Remember your best pal from highschool, Ethel Mae Praether? She still works at the bank. She's head cashier now. You may want to pay her a call while I run errands."

"Sure. I remember Ethel Mae. We had a lot in common. We were both tall and skinny and we both wore glasses. Back then it was common to say 'men never make passes at girls who wear glasses.' That didn't help my feelings one bit. Is she still flat as an ironing board?"

132

"She's well past puberty," Darcy laughed.

Ann continued her trip down memory lane. "She never wore make up and her hair was too thin! I know! We can gloat about our years of single independence. I can hardly wait!"

As they reached the edge of town and turned into Main Street, they noticed someone walking briskly along the sidewalk. The older man was dressed in faded blue overalls stretched over his expansive belly, with the sides unbuttoned for comfort. Dark splotches, obviously sweat stains on the back of his blue chambray shirt, were the mark of honest toil. Rolled back sleeves revealed large, hairy, sun-reddened forearms. A large floppy shapeless old straw hat with sweat stains about the band was pushed back from a broad, sunburned, cheerful face beaded with perspiration. In well-worn, dusty, high-top work shoes, he strode purposely along with something in his right hand. Closer inspection revealed the man held a large snake by the tail, a snake large as a man's arm and a good six feet long.

Anne's eyes widened and her jaw dropped as she stared at the scene.

"What is that fool doing?" she gasped.

"Oh, that's Doak Winters. He seems to have a snake."

"Why is he dragging that thing around with him! And in town!"

"It's a rattlesnake, obviously dead, so it can't hurt anyone. He probably found it on his property and wants to show it off."

"Somebody should call the police! This is awful!"

"It's his snake! He's not threatening anyone. He's taking it to show-and-tell at the spit-and-whittle bench in front of the post office. After he shows it off, he'll dispose of it."

"That is the reason I left this place! Who, in his right mind, would drag a snake down a public street! Who, indeed, unless he is crazy!"

"Doak's alright! That's just his way of being friendly. People know about snakes and stay away from their natural habitats. But when one invades your property, you have the right to defend yourself. He wouldn't bother, except this one looks extra-large and he wants to show it off. He didn't want to haul it in his car so he took it the only way he had."

"This is the stupidest conversation I ever had! I can hardly wait to get back to civilization!" Anne shuddered.

Darcy laughed and shook her head.

"I'll park in front of the bank while I do my errands."

Chapter Thirty

Ray lowered the newspaper. "Looks like George finally got off his duff and accomplished something. Quite a story in the paper about a sting operation right here! Can you believe all of that going on right under our noses? Makes me wonder, what took him so long?"

"This is exciting! Maybe folks will stop down-grading George Moran as sheriff. George has always been a good sheriff. It would be hard to find another as protective and caring as he is about our community. What else is in that story?"

"It says a boy named Max Thayer was the dealer. Isn't he the boy who drove the car the day Gaylene got in that scrape?"

"Max is the senior boy who wears designer jeans to school. There is a big distinction. He rides with the young man who drives the red Jaguar."

"Well, Max is locked up, charged with selling illegal drugs to minors. Somebody named Henderson is involved. Do we know any Hendersons? The boys are locked up but they won't talk, according to the paper. They both took the fifth. George says he has enough to send them up whether they talk or not."

"George may be bluffing. If those boys really are selling drugs, they may have enough money to hire a smart lawyer, a legal eagle to get them out on bail. George needs enough hard evidence to make a strong case before they walk. If they walk, they may run."

"Hello, George. I hear you are making progress with the drug problem."

"Hello, Darcy. Have a seat. Why yes! After we made a deal with

Jeff and his parents, we let him let out. Of course, he was guarded around the clock for his own protection. We sent one of the state boys with him, a young man who posed as a highschool boy. Jeff went back to that crowd at Marv's place. He told the other kids he was out on bail, the agent was his cousin from Houston, and they wanted to buy some hard stuff. It worked, except we only have Max for pushing and we don't have much on the Henderson boy. He was there with a large amount of drugs in his pockets but that's possession. Nobody saw him sell anything"

"Where is Jeff now?"

"We had to lock him up again. We told the press he was out on bail and got caught in the round-up from the sting. We have to keep him here until we get this cleaned up. It's for his own protection. We can defer his trial as long as we want. That will keep his name off permanent records."

"May I talk to him here? In your presence?"

Seeing Jeff brought in wearing handcuffs and escorted by an armed officer, Darcy felt her heart break. How could a nice kid like Jeff, with his potential and advantages, come to this?

"Mrs. Parker, I am working at doing things right. I did everything the sheriff told me to. Now they have two people locked up who were selling drugs to us. Did I do what I was supposed to?"

"Jeff, you have done a man's work. We're proud of you! What we need to know now, is there anything you can tell us about either of these boys? Anything about the way they operate?"

"I don't know either of them that well. I mean, they don't discuss business with me. I'm in the next cell but they talk in low tones. I can't hear what they are talking about."

"Are you afraid of either of them? Are you afraid to anger either of them? Do they seem mean or vicious or violent?"

"Mrs. Parker, I am really glad you brought that up. I am not nervous about Max. Not one bit. I wouldn't want to fight him but I don't think that would ever be necessary. Max has always been a nice guy and nice to me, except for selling drugs. But I am afraid of the other one, the one called Hank. I saw the arresting officers take a knife off him. There is only one reason to carry that long, sharp knife in his boot. He plans to use it on anybody who crosses him!"

"Do you think we could work a deal with Max? Do you think he would go for it or do you think he will hold out in loyalty to Henderson?"

"There's still some good left in Max. Maybe enough to help himself."

"George, how much longer can you hold them here legally?"

"Frankly, Darcy, all we have is dealing and possession, first offense, unless we come up with a better plan. With a good lawyer, they could come out with a suspended sentence and be right back here, dealing!"

"George, put those boys in separate cells. Keep them so far apart they cannot see each other or hear each other. I don't think you can ever break the older one. And he is older, regardless what he tells you, at least twenty-five. Put Jeff near Max. Maybe he can help us a bit. I'm betting Max is more scared than he admits. Jeff, you should drop a few little hints to Max. Let him think it over before you try to make a deal. George, don't let Max and Henderson near each other, even in the hall. If Jeff is afraid of Henderson, then so are the other boys. He sounds extremely dangerous!"

Darcy looked at Jeff, remembering a baby face and innocent brown eyes when he entered her first grade class. He was a well-behaved, docile boy, the kind you expect to see holding a good job and winning a beautiful girl. Seeing him in present surroundings made her heart ache but outward, she remained calm and brisk.

"Jeff, do you know what we need?"

"Yes, ma'am! You need Max to roll over and squeal on Hank. And you need me to sow a few seeds of doubt in Max's mind first, soften him up a bit before the sheriff calls him back in here to work a deal."

So much for maudlin thoughts of babyish faces, for they do grow up in a hurry, she thought ruefully. Aloud she remained brisk and business-like.

"You are right! Be very careful and move slowly. Whatever you do, do not mention that you already have a deal. Suggest to Max that the two of you could make a deal because you are both minors. 'Minor in possession' could walk if he had the right lawyer and the right jury. If Max shows any sign of giving you trouble, then you back off. If you feel like you should be moved away from there, tell the sheriff. Devise a signal. Right, George?"

"Darcy, we watch Jeff night and day, with cameras concealed in the cell block. With everything else going on around here, we don't need any more bad surprises. Jeff, we have to take you back there but don't advertise where you have been. If anyone asks, say we grilled you but you wouldn't crack."

After Jeff left the room, George shook his head as he spoke reluctantly. "Darcy, we sent that agent along with Jeff because he was small enough and looked young enough to be a teen. He's a rookie anxious to prove himself and he snapped the trap too soon. We don't have all we need to make a strong case against the Henderson boy. With a good lawyer claiming first offense, he could get off with deferred sentence. I need something else!"

"George, you may already have something else. Something you overlooked."

"Yeah, you are right! I must have missed something!"

"That camper trailer near the mobile home court! It showed up there about the time Faith disappeared. It has no ties to this community. It is apparently vacant. I want to know! Why is it there?"

In exasperation, George snapped. "Frankly, Darcy, who cares! Why do you think you care? It is just an old empty camper! Probably somebody left it there 'cause they were too lazy to haul it to the dump!"

"That was the Murphy property. When Mrs. Murphy died last year, she left it to her daughter, Addie Murphy Henderson, who lives in Lawton. Mrs. Henderson has one son. Isn't that young man sitting in your jail named Henderson?"

"Hmmm. Come to think of it, that trailer is parked illegally! No permit! Seems to be abandoned! We may need to make a case! Thanks, Darcy. Excuse me! I have calls to make!"

"Good Lord! George has really made headlines now! A big report in our local paper makes him a modern Wyatt Earp! He is also on the front page of the Daily Oklahoman. Listen to this, Darcy! 'Leading a daring day-time raid, Sheriff George Moran uncovered a meth lab in a most unlikely place. Taking a cue from the well-known classic, 'The Purloined Letter,' criminals concealed their activity right under the public nose. In a posh residential area of a sleepy little town in southern Oklahoma, the substance was made in dead of night, then sold to the children of unsuspecting townspeople. On a vacant lot, only a few feet from the curb, an apparently abandoned camper trailer proved to be the source of illegal drugs plaguing the community for months. Our hat is off to local Sheriff George Moran for diligence and perseverance. This same area a few weeks ago was also scene of another crime, the unsolved murder of sixteen-year-old Faith Brandon, which was drug related. Already in custody is Henry 'Hank' Henderson, Lawton, accused of possession of illegal drugs. Ownership of the camper has been traced directly to Adelia Henderson, Lawton.'

"Aren't you impressed, Darcy? I was beginning to lose faith in George but you were right all along. He was working, in his own way."

"Ray, if I tell you something, will you never repeat it?"

"Of course. Whatever are you talking about?"

"Jeff Vanault has been transferred to a detox unit. He was arrested but never formally charged. He is a minor and if he gets clean and stays clean, he will come out with a clean record. His lawyer told George he would have no trouble getting the armed robbery charge dropped. There were no weapons used and the grandmother refuses to testify against him. The bank robbery charge will be changed to breaking and entering because nothing was taken except that old safe. The banker agreed to drop all charges later, when Jeff completes detox. Can you live with that without ever telling anyone?"

"Why, Darcy, you know if you ask me to, I will never tell! But what's this got to do with the story in the paper?"

"Jeff was mixed up, confused, because of drugs. All this report in the paper about drugs made me think of it. I remember what a nice little boy he was and the promising future he had, before all that permissive parenting got in the way. He needed firm guidance from his parents instead of smothering permissiveness! By the way, Jeff plans to enter college and major in criminology and child psychology. He wants to go into law enforcement and work with juveniles. Isn't that wonderful?"

"That is certainly a switch! What came over him?"

"Maybe he underwent a conversion. I hope it takes. I hate to see one of my most promising pupils land in the state prison known as Big Mac."

"Darcy, we have been so involved with our neighbors, we haven't paid proper attention to our own affairs. It's not long until the hearing about your land. Have you given any thought to that?"

"Of course I have! But what can I do that hasn't already been done? I don't like to discuss it when James is around. He gets very agitated when we talk about it. I will not mention the name of the banker for fear James will retaliate, maybe do physical harm to the man. I thought to gloss over it in hope he forgets about it. Maybe he will decide to travel or he may decide to stay with one of my sisters."

Shaking his head, Ray replied, "Darcy, you are deceiving no one but yourself! James feels this is his home, because he lived here with your mother. It's obvious that his roots are here. That man is not going anywhere!

"Anne and Gussie were less than cordial when he returned, while you gave him a home. They remember him. You could not. Yet you took him in on faith. They don't want the responsibility of a sick old man with no place to go. In words of one syllable, they don't want to be saddled with him. You took him in with no questions asked. So basically, you are all he has! Why wouldn't he feel protective of you? Why would he leave?"

"I'm sorry for the trouble between him and Mama but it was their problem, not mine. I've lost Mama and no one can ever take her place. But I still have one parent, even though I don't know him well. It's no problem to have him here. He entertains himself. I see him only at meals and when we watch TV. By the way, we should put a TV in his room, like we did for Gaylene. I'm sure our choice of programs is not always his taste. Back to your original question. If we discuss the case, we should take a drive or a walk. I don't like to discuss it when James can overhear."

"I don't understand! Whatever do you mean?"

"He gets very fierce and protective when someone threatens his baby girl. I don't like to agitate him. He has ears like a lynx. One never knows how much he overhears. Would you like to show me the new calves in the back pasture? I have time before Gaylene comes home from school."

Chapter Thirty-One

"Ray, will you step outside with me? I want to show you the moon."

Ray promptly accompanied his wife to the front porch before asking in a low voice, "What are you up to, Darcy? The moon won't be full for two weeks."

"The Lassiters are at it again!"

"Good Lord! You're right! Except they're even louder!"

"She's screaming! What is she saying! Can you understand?"

"About something is nobody's business. She can do as she pleases."

"Can you see them? With the drapes open, it's like a movie. There! She left the room. I am amazed to see how fast she can move! Her size astounds me! What do those men see in a woman who weighs three hundred and fifty pounds?"

"You wouldn't understand. It is just something men do, like taking drink when they know they shouldn't. Like speeding up when someone tries to cut in front of you. Men have a hard time backing away from a challenge, even when they know results can be disastrous. There! What he is doing? He is going into the closet, reaching to the shelf. What in the world?"

"Ray, is that a gun? Yes! I am sure that's a gun! Clint Lassiter, the gentlest man I know! I don't believe this!"

"Darcy, he had a gun and he followed Nora! I'll walk out there!"

"You will stay home and call the sheriff! It's not smart to interfere in domestic disturbance, especially when firearms come into the act."

"I don't hear anything now. Do you think they called off

hostilities?"

They both stiffened when a piercing scream ripped the quiet evening. They could see Nora Lassiter racing through the house, followed by her enraged husband. A shot was followed by two more shots fired close together.

"Now it's time to call George!" Ray exclaimed as he raced to the phone.

As he used his gavel, the judge looked about the room.

"The hearing to gather information on the deaths of Clint and Nora Lassiter is open. Please come to order! We will hear from Sheriff Moran first."

After the sheriff was seated, the justice spoke. "We will be as informal as the law allows. Sheriff, will you please tell us your account of this event."

"At nine o'clock last night, I had a call from Ray Parker, saying he could hear a loud disturbance at the Lassiter house near him. I went by Ray's house first and asked him to go along with me. When we got there, Clint was standing in the front yard, staring at the sky. We turned into his drive and drove to the house. We could see Clint, over to the side, just standing there looking at the sky, like he was checking the weather. We drove right up beside him and stopped. When I spoke to him, he just stared at me. Acted like he wanted to speak but couldn't.

"I got out of the car and walked toward him. That's when he held up that pistol in his right hand. I hadn't realized he had a gun. I stopped and stood still because I didn't want to excite him. He stared at the gun a long minute. Then he raised it to his temple and fired. Judge, he never said one word to either of us!

"We went inside and found his wife face down on the floor in the hall. She was dead with a bullet wound in the back of her head and two more in her back. It was obviously murder-suicide."

"Ray, I will never understand why people who tire of a marriage take bizarre methods of retaliation. If Nora were unhappy, why didn't she leave? Why abase Clint with her outlandish behavior? What did she hope to accomplish?"

"Darcy, you asked a question that has plagued couples and marriage counselors since marriage was invented. Have Clint's children have been notified?"

"Yes, of course. I have reached a decision. I will never tell either of them what led up to this. We are the only people who know about her infidelities. I've never breathed a word of this to a living soul. At first, I felt if I told, she would believe the outcome was my fault. After thinking about it, I concluded that I really had no reason to mention it to anyone. It isn't my business or yours.

"She changed personalities since we were all friends. Whatever happened to her, whatever the experts choose to call it— depression, irreparable differences, mid-life crisis, temporary insanity, makes no difference now. Those nice children of theirs should never know the ugly truth. If they knew, they would have to carry the burden for the rest of their lives. I will never tell them that their mother's wanton philandering drove their father into a jealous, murderous rage!"

Chapter Thirty-Two

"Darcy, I really don't want to!"

"Come on, Ray! You'll like it!"

"There is no guarantee that I will!"

"Please, Ray. It takes two. I can't do it without you."

"Darcy! It simply will not work!"

"Ray, a negative attitude never helps. Cooperation is the key word here."

James stopped in the doorway to stare, to put his hands on his hips and shake his head in disbelief.

"Will someone tell me what is going on? Or is this a private subject not meant for my delicate ears?"

Ray, red-faced, turned away to retrieve the newspaper he had discarded. Darcy laughed before explaining to her father.

"Dad, I want to learn square dancing and Ray has his heels in the ground. He won't budge."

James shook his head again as he looked thoughtfully at his son-in-law. Then he, too, laughed.

"Is that all! Ray, it will not hurt you to learn something new! It will open new avenues for you. Think about it, Ray! New ideas, new people, new places to go! Did you ever try square dancing?"

Grudgingly, "No."

"Tell me your main objection to learning."

"I don't think I can do it! It looks complicated! People will laugh at me!"

"I asked for one reason. I got three. I think the last one listed is the true one. Will it help if I tell you that I can square dance? It requires concentration but it's not complicated. If it were, how many people would be involved in it? Children can square dance. We used to call it folk dancing because it was all ages, even entire families, dancing together."

"Okay. I have an idea. Maybe you would dance with Darcy."

"Ray, that is not the point. Darcy wants to dance with you. Has she ever asked you to do anything that embarrassed you?"

"Well, no. But this is different."

Darcy intercepted, "Ray, please see this from my view point. A class starts at the college next week and we should start at the beginning. I promise, if one person laughs at you, I will deck him! If it's obviously too much for us, I'll be first to say 'Quit.' But it won't hurt us to try! We need a diversion, something to balance out all the trauma in our life lately. Even if you don't need it, I do! Please try, for my sake!"

"We-ell, all right. Since you put it that way, I'll try. Don't be surprised if I fall down and break a leg the first night!" was the gloomy forecast.

James looked up from his book as two smiling people entered the den. "Well, here are our students! Ray, I see you're still standing on two good legs and obviously in good spirits. I have to know, how many people laughed at you?"

"Dad, nobody laughed at anybody. It's a class! It's a nice group of well-behaved adults with an excellent teacher. But there was a problem! Every woman there wanted to dance with Ray! They were almost fighting each other to grab him for a partner. That is the reason he had so much fun!" Darcy teased.

"I thought you were all set to deck anyone who misbehaved."

"We were having too much fun for that. I laughed until my sides ache. How about you, Ray?"

A long thoughtful moment was followed by a shy grin.

"Nice group! I liked everybody there! It was great! We might as well stay in the class."

"Dad, it was great! A bit strenuous but we'll get used to that. I can hardly wait til we can go to the dances and wear a standard costume. I have a million ideas for dress designs. I can hardly wait to try some of them!"

Ray shook his head before dissolving into laughter.

"One lesson and she's wild for new clothes! I can already see what my life will be."

"Yes, indeed! The couples dress like Bobsy Twins. Your costume matches mine so I will learn to make Western shirts. It's great fun and I'm glad we are in it. We need something light. I think you should join us, Dad. You need to mix with others. How about asking Grace Coombs to be your partner?"

"Do you mean to drag me into this?"

"Why not? You were very persuasive at coaxing Ray. You should repeat your sales talk to yourself. You spend too much time alone. It wouldn't hurt a thing for you to take someone to dinner once in awhile. I'll call Grace and ask her to attend lessons with us next week. Then you can take it from there. I am sure you remember how," Darcy teased as she left the room.

Chapter Thirty-Three

The courtroom was filled to capacity. Latecomers sought seats in the already crowded balcony. Attorneys entered to seat themselves at tables facing the bench. The day before had been spent in jury selection, now seated in the jury box. At last armed deputies escorted the accused, seating each with their separate attorneys. They removed their handcuffs, then seated themselves nearby to remain alert and watchful.

The bailiff stood and sang out in a strong melodious bass, "All rise!"

Rustling and scraping accompanied the response as the judge appeared. With a commanding air, he strode purposely into the room, his robe regally flowing about him. As he seated himself, the bailiff's musical voice commanded, "Be seated," allowing them to return to their seats.

From the third row, Ray and Darcy awaited the trial of the century, for the town, for the entire county, of the young men accused of selling drugs.

The charges were read. The sheriff took the stand and was sworn. He told the circumstance of their arrest. Evidence and pictures enforced his testimony. The investigating agent for the state was seated and sworn. He told essentially the same story as the sheriff. The young men had indeed been caught in the act of selling drugs to minors. So far, it was routine, open-and-shut.

Darcy gave long, searching looks at the accused. Max Thayer sat with head ducked, staring at his hands, his young face a mixture of red-faced shame and defiance, a normal reaction for an inexperienced boy.

Darcy chanced a good view of Hank Henderson. From a distance he looked like a choirboy, round bland face, china blue eyes, angelic smile, blond hair neatly styled. But when she chanced to look into his eyes, a chilling horror washed over her, for pure hate and venom met her gaze. She had looked into the soul of a psychopath. Shivering, she moved nearer to Ray.

The sheriff was recalled to tell of his deductions regarding the old camper.

"It appeared there mysteriously. Couldn't find one person who knew anything about it. Never anyone around it. Nobody living in it. We couldn't find anyone responsible for it. It appeared to be abandoned. After we search it, we found it to be a meth lab. By checking public records, we found the camper is registered by Adelia Murphy Henderson, of Lawton. So is the lot it's parked on.

"We questioned Mrs. Henderson. At first she said she gave her old camper to her son to use as a fishing camp on the lake. But when we told her what it was being used for, she clammed up and refused to tell us anything. That's okay. We already had her son locked up for possession. Now we have tied him to a meth lab. The charges against Henderson are manufacture and distributing a controlled substance."

At this point, an argument broke out between Max Thayer and his attorney. It grew louder while all eyes focused on them. The judge asked the attorney, "Is there a problem with your client?"

"Your Honor, my client wants to take the stand. I have advised him not to. In spite of counsel, he insists."

"Young man, stand up!" the judge ordered.

Max rose to stand, pale, shaking, holding the edge of the table for support.

The judge continued. "Do you understand that you do not have to testify at all? The state has charged you with the crime of selling drugs. The state must prove this charge beyond the shadow of a doubt while you do not have to say anything. You do not have to take the stand and you do not have to say a word. You should be aware that if you do take the stand, you may incriminate yourself. Even worse, you will subject yourself to questions by the prosecution. If that occurs, you are bound by law to answer truthfully. Perjury, lying under oath, is a crime punishable by imprisonment. Do you understand what I say?"

"Your honor, I do understand every word! I am the only one who knows what really happened. I want to talk! I have to talk! I have to tell people what really went on! I want the truth to go into the record!"

"Do you understand that you may incriminate yourself? If you do, you will have to take the consequences!"

"Yes, your honor. I know all of that. This trial is a farce if I don't tell. People have a right to know!"

"Then, by all means, take the stand. Sheriff, we will continue with your report later. You may step down."

Max was immediately sworn and seated When questioned as to age, occupation, and home address, he replied,

"Seventeen, I go to school, and I live with my mother on Birch street. Your Honor, I want the people in this town to know, I never meant things to go this far! Yes, I sold drugs! When I started selling marijuana to the other kids, I needed money. My father died when I was small and my mother has a hard time paying our bills. It seemed harmless because that stuff is available to kids anyway! Those who want it have no trouble finding it. I might as well have the profit.

"Before I knew it, I was in too deep and couldn't get out. I was dealing hard stuff for Hank! He would not let me out! Every time I tried to quit, he threatened me. Your Honor, he said he would fix me! Fix me for good if I quit him! I knew about that knife he carried. I knew he'd hurt my mother if I made him really mad! All I could hope for was to finish school and move away to some place where he would never find me.

"Then Faith Brandon got into the picture. I wasn't dealing to her. Hank was. At first he gave her marijuana, just one or two now and then. Before long he moved her onto the heavy stuff. After she was hooked, he began charging her. He made her pay up front and she didn't have that kind of money.

"She was a kid! She made good grades and planned to go to college. She had a nice boy friend but of course it wasn't long before he found out about the drugs. They had a big fight about that and broke up. Faith didn't have any money so she started having sex with Hank to pay for drugs.

"Hank never went near that old camper in daytime. He waited til after midnight to cook off his meth. Faith knew what time he would show up at the camper so she waited til her mother went to sleep. Then she slipped out and walked across vacant property, only a half-mile, to the camper. She had sex with Hank, got her fix and enough to get through the week, then walked back home.

"One night Hank got her drunk and high at the same time. She was a mess! Bawling! Tears and snot running down her face! Screaming at him! Telling him she'd get off drugs and turn him in. She said she wanted the world to know what he did to her! Judge, she told him that every time she came to his trailer! But she always came back!

"'Bout that time, I walked in. I knew when she slept it off, she wouldn't remember any of it. But she would not shut up! Hank was afraid someone would hear her, so he got mad and started beating her. At first he just slapped her around a little. She still wouldn't shut up, so he really got riled up. He punched her with his fists! He kept on hitting, trying to make her shut up. He hit her so hard, she passed out. At first, he thought she was dead! She was breathing but she was really out!

"Then he got worried about what would happen the next day when she showed up with two black eyes and a bruised face. A little fib about 'falling out of bed' or 'bumped into a door' wouldn't work. What if her mother took her to a doctor and the doctor found she was on drugs? She'd tell for sure then.

"When he couldn't wake her up, he picked her up and pitched her into his car. She was not very big and she was out cold! He could pitch her around like a rag doll. I thought he meant to take her home. We could sneak her back into her house with no problem and let her handle the bruised face.

"Then he pulled a gun on me! At gun point, he made me get into the car. He drove to that bridge where they found Faith. He held the gun on me and made me get out. I had to stand where he could see me while he dragged Faith to the railing.

"He stood her up on the railing. She had no idea what she was doing but she did it somehow! While she stood there, all wobbly and limp, he shot her in the head, Judge!

"She fell off the bridge and he emptied his gun into her after she was already dead! He said if I ever told, he'd kill me! I knew he would, too! Judge, I've never been so scared! I feared for my life! I feared what he could do to my mother! I know he's mean enough to burn our house with her in it.

"When he gets mad, he's crazy mad! And mean with it! I've seen his tantrums. He'd rage and scream as he drove along the street, shootin' dogs just sittin' in their own yards!

Judge, I'm mortally afraid of him, for myself and for my mother! I never dared tell any of this until now!"

For a brief moment, total silence reigned. Then a buzzing rush of whispers combined with reporters racing from the room, cell phones at the ready.

Max's attorney seized the moment to shout, "Your Honor, I demand that all charges against my client be dismissed!"

"Order in the court!" said the judge as he banged his gavel.

A total waste of breath, as the good people of the town were aghast, agog, shocked out of their usual decorum and not inclined to pay any attention as the judge pounded his useless gavel. Neighbor chattered excitedly to other neighbors. Aggie Brandon burst into tears and several hands reached out to comfort her.

Ray and Darcy sat stunned until Darcy avowed loudly,

"I was right about that camper! There was no good reason for it being there!"

Ray burst into laughter as he gave his wife a quick one-armed hug. "Honey, the older you get, the more like your mother you are! Let's go home! I'm sure court is over for the day. I thought I heard him say, 'Court is recessed.' Yes! There goes the judge! He probably wants to lie down with a cold cloth on his brow! He's had a big day and it isn't even noon!"

At home, they interrupted each other with comments about the trial and the outcome.

What a relief! It's over! At last! The terrible mystery of Faith is over! Poor Faith! Poor Aggie! Poor, foolish little girl! If only she had told someone!

"One of Mama's favorite quotes was 'Oh, what a tangled web we weave, When first we practice to deceive!'

"Darcy, you were right! You were right all along! You said drugs came first. Everything else stemmed from that. It was obvious to you from the start."

"I like to take first things first. I'm truly sorry about Faith! But her death was not the catalyst that started this nightmare! The drugs came first, creeping in like a bad smell! My only comfort is that other girls may learn the obvious lesson. The first exciting experience with drugs starts one on a downhill path. If nothing else comes of this, let's hope other children learn from Faith's mistakes. What a terrible object lesson!"

Chapter Thirty-Four

"Ray, will you place the extra leaf in the dining table, please? Do you think Gaylene suspects anything?"

"Honey, what difference can it make now? Surprise parties are a big waste of time. Why not let them enjoy the anticipation?"

"I thought she might get suspicious when we all went along for her driving test this morning. I knew she would ace the test but I wanted to be there and see her face when she received her license. James felt the same way. And well he should. This was his project. The picture you snapped of her as the trooper presented her license is definitely a keeper!"

"She had a full escort. I doubt if our own child ever commanded more attention than she has today. It was clever of you to suggest that she drive to Doris Lee's house her first time out with a license."

"I had Doris Lee on alert. She will keep Gaylene there til time for the party. She will suggest a movie and they will come back here so Gaylene can change. While she changes, we sneak the young people into the dining room."

At that moment the two girls entered the kitchen. Neither seemed to notice that Ray and Darcy abruptly stopped talking.

"We're going to a movie after we eat," Gaylene reported on her way to her room. "It's okay, isn't it? Coming, Doris Lee?"

When she returned, Darcy asked, "Gaylene, will you look in the dining room to see if I remembered napkins?"

The chorus of "SURPRISE!" rang through the house to signal Darcy, Ray, and James to join in.

"I thought you should have a Sweet Sixteen party, Gaylene! Getting your driver license is not enough!"

Gaylene, big brown eyes shining and a smile to light a church, gasped,"Aunt Darcy! It really is a surprise! I love it, love it, love it!"

"Let's move to the backyard. We have hot dogs, potato salad, lemonade. And a huge birthday cake later. Have you seen it?"

"It's beautiful! Did you make it?"

"Of course! Homemade cakes taste better! Now take your friends out and entertain them! Ray cooks the dogs while everybody makes his own. We open gifts when we cut the cake."

When everyone had his fill of picnic supper and the cake had been served, Ray presented a small gaily wrapped parcel to the honoree. Gaylene unwrapped it to reveal a small wallet.

"Ooh! I see a couple of twenties in there. Wow! That rates a hug, Ray."

"Good place to carry your new license, too."

James came forward with smaller package, a key ring with one key. A tab displayed the initial "G."

"You may drive my car, Gaylene, but you must always ask first. Okay?"

"Of course, I will! A generous offer, indeed! You have a beautiful car! I promise to be very careful when I drive it. A hug for you, James. You are my surrogate grandfather! Without you, this day would be entirely different."

After gifts were opened and properly admired, Darcy suggested they move to the den.

"Roll up the rugs and dance! Records are over there. If you need anything, we're in the kitchen."

They made their way along the hall to seat themselves at the kitchen table. Darcy smiled and said,"I left my gift on her bed. I gave her some pretty pajamas. She's gained a tiny bit of weight and I am tired of those old baggy things she wears. Ray, did you notice? Gaylene ate a hot dog! She ate a piece of her cake and ice cream! Did you notice that?"

"Now that you mention it, she did, with a hearty appetite! You can take a bow for that. Gaylene has made some big changes since she came here. It's good to see her eating and laughing and acting like a normal teenager."

"She laughs! She talks, actually carries on a normal conversation! Not a bit like the little mouse who moved in with us. It's just as well our doctor never found a specialist for her. She needed a lot of love. Above all, she needs a family and needs to feel like she fits in."

Ray's eyes shone with affection as he leaned over to kiss her. "You've certainly done all of that! She found a home and she knows it! And we have three pretty daughters! The party's a great hit! Now you have done enough. You sit here while I clean up the grill. I may even find a hot dog for Buddy. It is dog-eat-dog around here!"

The serene Sunday afternoon offered a picture of domestic bliss. Ray read the sports page with stocking feet on the hassock while he watched TV baseball. James had retired for his nap. Darcy was reading. A smiling Gaylene settled beside Darcy on the couch and leaned against her.

"Aunt Darcy, at the party last night, Benny Watson asked me to go to a movie with him Saturday night. Is that okay?"

"Tell me about Benny Watson."

"I like him. I like him because he's clean, with himself and his language. He's smart but not smart aleck. He makes good grades, he's in band, on the basketball team, had the lead in the senior play. Oh, yes! He plans to go to Oklahoma State."

"Wow! If I were interviewing, I'd hire him on the spot. Now tell me, what do you really like about him?"

"He's always nice to me and he treats me like a lady. We never run out of things to talk about but he never talks trash. He likes to laugh and when he laughs, that makes me laugh. He has a nice smile and I like to dance with him."

"We-e-ll, Gaylene, if you don't want see a movie with him, I shall! He certainly sounds too good to pass up! Call the movie theater, ask what time the movie ends and we'll talk about curfew. Okay?"

"Oka-ay! I think I'll give Buddy a good bath and get him all spruced up! I want Benny to like him, too. We'll be in the back yard."

After she left the room, Darcy grinned at Ray. "Most girls try new hair styles to impress a first date. She grooms her dog. That's what I call a clean-living gal!"

Just then Gaylene raced across the yard to shout into the open window, "Ray! An airplane is circling this house! Come and look!"

Shoving his feet into his shoes, he hurried out with trailing shoestrings to see a small plane was indeed circling his house. At a window of the plane, a face appeared, a voice called, "Ray! Follow us!"

Darcy came to the door to ask, "Ray, what is happening?"

"That's Zack! He's going to land! Hop in!"

"Gaylene, that is Ray's crazy brother! He's dropping in, literally. Want to go along? Can you leave your dog?"

"It's okay. I haven't started his bath. I want to go!"

They raced to Ray's truck and leaped in as Ray started the motor. They left the drive to turn into the county road. The small plane waggled its wings and moved away. Passing clumps of big trees, they crossed an old bridge with tall, rusty banisters, to round a curve and enter a treeless stretch of level road. The plane turned and swooped down to land on the road not far ahead of them. Ray braked to a stop but left the motor running as the plane sped toward him. As it stopped a few feet from his bumper, he turned off the motor with a sigh of relief.

"Whew! I wasn't sure he could stop in time! What would my insurance company say if I filed an accident report of a head-on crash with a small plane?"

A door of the plane opened to allow Zack's athletic figure a graceful exit. He hurried to Ray with movie star smile and hand extended. After they shook hands, bear-hugged, then pounded each other on the back for awhile, Zack turned to Darcy.

"Darcy, you take good care of him! He looks great! You, too! Oho! Who is this?"

"Gaylene, this is Ray's brother, Zack. Gaylene Haines lives with us. She's part of the family now. Are you Zack or Uncle Zack?"

"Zack will do. My friend, Lon Hughes. Got anything to drink at the house? Flying makes me thirsty!"

"Let's go back to the house for shade and lemonade."

"First, we move the plane off the highway. Let's move it over to this level spot so people can pass. We won't be gone long. We fly daylight only."

Later that evening in their bedroom, Darcy asked, "What did Zack want? I know he didn't fly up here just to impress us. He never bothers about us unless he's in trouble or wants to show off. Exactly what does he want?"

"Darcy, can't Zack drop in for a friendly chat?"

"Ray, cut to the chase. Zack shows up when he wants something."

"He and his friend plan to raise emus."

"Want to expand on that? Zack does not own land and those big birds take space. Does he want money?"

"In their scheme, they furnish the birds and the feed while I furnish the land and labor. We would each have one third of the profit."

"Providing there is a profit! Meanwhile, you do all the work in all kinds of weather! Emus are risky business. Many people try it and lose their collective shirt. What did you say?"

"That relatives should not go into business together. It leads to other issues. I told him his offer is strictly for the birds! I'm a cow man! But they were nice enough to offer me a ride in the plane before they left. I took Gaylene along, a big thing for her. She had a lot of firsts for her birthday."

They had just fallen to sleep when the telephone woke them. Ray answered and after a brief conversation he swung his feet out of bed and reached for his clothes.

Darcy sat up to ask, "Was that one of our daughters?"

"Zack's wife. The plane crashed on landing. Both men are in the hospital. Zack asked for me. I have to go."

"How badly was he injured?"

"He's okay except his right hand is mangled. They are waiting for a surgeon. They may have to take it off. I have to go! I'll call when I know anything."

Chapter Thirty-Five

"Hello."

"Augusta? It's Darcy. I called to say I'm thinking about you."

"Darcy, I am truly glad to hear from you! And I have news! We have heard from Jon!"

"Tell me. Is he happy in his new life?"

"He checked out gay bars, trying to fit in. It's not as much fun as he expected. It takes money to hang out in gay bars, to drink and be available. He's older than most of them so they call him 'the old man.' That does not help!

"He had a good job with the telephone company. He worked there a long time and would have had a nice pension on retirement. But he quit his job and lost that. Now he wants it back. His old boss won't take him back at work and refuses to give him a reference. He's out of money and he wants to come home."

"How does Ellen feel about that?"

"She is very calm, like she expected this. She told him to get tested for AIDS and other sexually transmitted diseases and then call her. She won't let him in the house without written proof that he's clean. Says that would pose a hazard for her and their kids. She got a big promotion at work, meaning she can carry house payments and keep both kids in college. The kids work part time jobs and keep decent grades. They are terribly hurt and angry with their father. They feel that they were deserted, too. They advise Ellen to refuse him. She says she can survive without him but it's his house and he needs a place to live. If he comes back, they may try to work out an agreement they can both live with."

"Sounds like they're moving in that direction."

"I would feel the same way. If someone I loved and had children with was broke and homeless, I'd give him a place to live. If she takes him back, it will be a long time before the kids forgive him. They're hurt. Ellen is hurt. Now he is sorry! Deep down, I think he is sorriest of all over his pension!"

"He should have considered that before he quit his job! He may have legal recourse about his job. He should consult an attorney about getting re-instated at work. He did a foolish thing that he may never live down. They need family counseling. It bothers me when long-time marriages fail."

"Darcy, it bothers everybody. How are your bunch?"

Chapter Thirty-Six

"Darcy, there has been a jail break! In this little town where nothing ever happens! This is big!"

"Someone walked away from trash pick up?"

"No. It's Hank Henderson, the dope dealer who killed Faith!"

"I thought he went to prison! How did he get out?"

"The prison is over-crowded so they had to hold him here until there was room for him. Today he overpowered the jailer who brought his lunch. He had been quiet all along, a model prisoner, really calm, docile, no problem. When the jailer brought his lunch tray today, he lay still, like he was unconscious. The jailer thought he was in bad trouble, maybe a case of drug overdose. So he unlocked the door and walked over to have a look at him. When he bent over to get a good look, Hank grabbed him, got his gun, and was out of there like a shot. His mother was parked outside, waiting, and they were out of town before the jailer could get his gag off. It was well-planned."

"It's straight out of the Old West! Where do they think they can go, with television, cell phone, computer, highway patrol with radar, road blocks, helicopters, stun guns, and trained dogs?"

"Tell that to the Hendersons. They have disappeared without a trace. I want you to stay inside and keep the doors locked."

"Why would they come here? It's silly to hang around here, with everybody nervous and alert. They are probably two states away by now."

"Maybe so. It was silly to break out of jail but that didn't stop him! I'm staying right here, in the house, with the TV on in case of a bulletin. With the Lassiters gone, we have no near neighbors. Out here in the country, if our phone line is cut, we are easy prey. I will not leave my wife and my home at the mercy of scum! If they get in here, they could stay for days. They could shoot us all and steal a car that would pass any search point. I am not moving!"

The tall, gangling woman narrowed eyes already narrow to glare at her son."Hank! Do you know what you're doing? Why are we here?"

"Aw, Maw, relax! The game refuge is the last place the law will look for us! If we stay on the freeway, or even on regular highways, some hotshot cop will spot us. Road blocks, an army of snipers, the whole shooting match is out in force. We won't get twenty miles! The only way is to find an out of the way place to hole up. When the cops get tired of looking for us, we can find an easy road to get away from here. We need to think about an old oil field road or an old farm road that's unhandy for most folk. Did you bring a map of the county?"

"I went to the library and found one that shows old roads from years ago. You're sure about this? You don't think they'll search the game refuge?'

"If we don't attract attention, they won't come near us. They will cover freeways and main highways. They will suppose we got away fast enough to miss the first road block, maybe two, and are miles away. Nobody ever comes out here except fishermen and bird watchers. In a word, retirees! The law doesn't care about old coots who have nothing to do but fish. Camping is not allowed here but fishing is okay. But there is no sentry of any kind at the entrance. Nobody counts the cars coming in or going out. If somebody stays behind, nobody is the wiser! We can stay as long as we don't attract attention. I said to bring plenty of staples, water, and sleeping bags. Okay?"

"It ain't fancy but we can eat for days on what's in the trunk of my car. This will be on the news, along with a good description of my car. That means my car is bound to attract attention. I couldn't think of any way to change its looks. So just exactly how are you planning to get out of here?"

"I'll park your car behind some brush. We can move two or three times daily if there is a lot of traffic around us. Likely there won't be. There are all sorts of places out here to conceal a car. We pretend to fish while we think about ways to leave. We carry binoculars, like bird watchers. Or we stay in the brush and be quiet. We need to plan on a couple of weeks here, at least. By that time, they'll be looking for us in Canada or Mexico. Did you bring extra clothes? I'll need a razor."

"Yes! Yes! I brought everything you asked! I even brought a few books, portable radio, paper and pens. A few things to help pass the time."

"We can use the radio to check on the cops but I don't plan to sit around reading. I'll move around, checking other visitors here. When someone comes in with a likely vehicle, that's time to move. We have to stay packed up tight, ready to go!"

"What about game rangers, park workers? Won't they ask questions?"

"I'll stay in heavy brush nearby, where I can see and hear. If somebody gets nosy, you say you came out here to look at wild flowers and take pictures. You're car won't start and you are just getting over a broken ankle, can't walk any distance. Tell them you've had a light stroke and are real easy to get disoriented. Act like you have a hearing problem. Act stupid. That shouldn't be a problem for you. I'll stay in the brush, close enough to see and hear but not visible to them. Our pictures are all over TV, plus a description of your car. If we're seen together, along with your car, somebody could recognize us."

"I took the tag off my car and put it in the toolbox. Nobody got our tag number."

"Good Lord! How did you miss getting stopped by the cops?"

"I replaced it with one I found at the salvage yard. Figured nobody would notice as long as I drove the right speed."

At the breakfast table, Darcy asked, "Ray, how long must we remain prisoners in our own home? It's been a week, with no trace of them. I think it's ironic that prisoners remain at large while we are forced to stay locked inside."

"Well, maybe we can relax just a little. But no getting separated for long periods of time! We need to stay within close distance of each other, in sight range or voice range. With most hostage situations, it usually starts as divide and conquer. I need to go out and check the cattle. I'll take the cell phone with me and I will be watchful to the utmost. Now you two stay close to each other and I'll be back soon."

Dawn, murky and drab, revealed moisture-laden clouds hanging low, giving the impression they could rake your hat off. Hank Henderson waked to stretch lazily in his sleeping bag. Early dawn was evidenced by a chorus of wild birds and chattering squirrels while a pair of jack rabbits scampered nearby. As he stretched luxuriously, water dripped from branches overhead to land on his face. He wiped water from his face and sat up to survey the day with a heavy lump in his chest. In haste, he rose to walk quietly to where his mother slept. He squatted near her and spoke softly.

"Hey, Ma! Wake up! We have to make plans."

The tall, bony form stiffened as narrow eyes opened to a squint.

"Ma, this time of year, it's warm and dry. We never planned on bad weather! We can't stay out here in the rain! Won't be any fishermen out in this! If park workers or game rangers happen by, we'll stand out like hens at a hawk convention. I meant to wait at least another week and then take a car from some old geezer out here fishing. Everybody stayed in today on account of rain! No cars to choose from! Not one! Get up! We have to change plans!"

"I'm awake! I think as well in a dry sleeping bag as standing in the rain! What's on your mind?"

"It's been a week. Plenty of time to cool off the cops. They have to get back to normal duty sometime. By now they may think we are in Montana, hanging out with D.B. Cooper. We need to split up. You will be safer without me and you don't want to go where I am going! We should dress and put all our things in the car. Don't leave anything that can be traced to us. I'll bury our trash and cover it over with brush."

"That's okay. You said to keep things packed tight and be ready to move on moment's notice. We're packed. What next?"

"Let's get changed. Did you bring two dresses like I said?"

"Well, of course, but I can only wear one. Why two?"

"Watch me! I always thought this would be a perfect way to confuse the cops. First, I need a tee shirt and panty hose. Trousers next and roll them up, like this! Now, a dress, wig and hat. When I switch back, I strip off the wig and dress. I can change my looks in two minutes. Where's that razor?"

"Now I see! Hey! This is great! Let me help you. You need a bit of blemish cream where your beard is. Now! That's better! Let's decide which wig. Are you blonde or brunette?"

"You have dark hair, Ma, so you should be blond. Won't matter for me. Should be long enough to flop around and cover part of my face. I think I'll try the longer one with heavy bangs. How's this?"

"Hey! If I didn't know, I'd take you for a woman! Is my wig on straight? Now try walking. That can be a give-away. This is important! Keep your knees together like a woman walks. I brought flat shoes for both of us. Heels could be a problem if we have to run. Ugh! Lordy, Lordy! Son! Good thing you're not looking for a date! You have lousy legs!"

"Ma! Shut up! Stay serious! Remember! If we're stopped, we are sisters, going to a third sister's funeral. We're both terribly upset so we keep the hankies ready. With wigs and hankies to wipe tears, it would be hard to say what we look like. If it's a bad situation, we cover our faces and bawl, loud! Men can't stand to hear a woman bawl.

"Now, let's get out of here! I'll drive you to the next town that's large enough to have a bus station. I'll park near the bus station but we won't be seen together. Buy a ticket to the next big town. When you get there, buy another one to where your sister lives. When you get there, don't say one word, to her or anybody, about any of this. Just say you miss her and don't have much to do at home. If you leave her place, don't go home. They'll watch our place 'til it rots down. I can travel faster alone and you have a better chance without me. I'll stay low profile and drive on back roads til I can steal a car. They will be watching the Mexican border so I'll try for Canada. Just don't go back home, not for a long time! If you run out of money and have to get a job, work as a housekeeper or nanny. Something that keeps you away from the public eye. Okay?"

"Anything suits me, Son, if it keeps you from taking the big needle!"

"I won't contact you and you must not contact me! If I try to contact you, I won't write. I'll call on your cell phone but not soon. It's too easy to trace a phone call or a postmark. Just tell yourself that no news is good news. We must not contact each other. Can you handle that?"

"Like I said, I can handle anything that helps you. Now let's go. We are using up daylight!"

When James entered the house with a strange woman by his side, Darcy was more than surprised. James hurried with introductions.

"Darcy, I went for a walk and right out front, I found this lady with a flat tire and no spare. Ma'am, my daughter, Darcy Parker. I forgot your name. I'm doing good these days to remember my own," he laughed ruefully.

"I'm Edie Ames," the stranger looked at her shoes as she murmured shyly in a hoarse whisper.

"How can we help you?" asked Darcy.

With downcast eyes, the woman replied in her shy way, "Like the man said, I only have three tires. I'm on my way to a funeral. I could still make it if I could catch a bus right away. Or maybe a plane. Is there an airport near here? I must have taken a wrong turn! I am totally lost! I need to be in Norman at four o'clock today. Is there any way to get there from here?"

The woman had kept her head lowered demurely but as she uttered the question, she looked straight into Darcy's eyes. Darcy was struck by the cold light in china blue eyes, eyes like frozen steel. Where had she seen eyes like that before?

James spoke. "Norman is only an hour away. Perhaps I could

drive you there. What do you think, Daughter?"

Darcy, frozen with fright and despair, remembered all too well where she had seen those eyes. In the courtroom as the accusation of 'murder' rang across the room! She had a killer right in her home!

She took a deep breath and managed to smile as she told the woman firmly, "My father is not strong. His gallantry overreaches his strength. He has health problems and we don't allow him to tax himself. I can call a repairman for your car. One of our local men brings an air tank with him. He fixes tires and refills them on the spot!"

"I'm sure that tire is ruined. I'll need time to shop for a tire and have it mounted. Right now, I want to attend my sister's funeral. Time is a factor."

"I have an idea!" Darcy offered brightly. "My friend is driving there today. He drives each week to Oklahoma City and passes right through Norman. Wait here! I know I can find transportation for you! "

There was a phone in the den but Ray had carelessly pitched the morning paper over it. Taking a cue from that, and hoping it wouldn't ring, Darcy left to use the kitchen phone. Willing her hands not to shake, she dialed the number for George Moran's office. When he answered, she spoke clearly and slowly.

"George, this is Darcy Parker. I need a favor from you today! Right now! This minute! Do you hear me? George, I need your help now!"

From the other end of the line, George replied, "Uuuh, Darcy, is there a problem at your house? Do you need help from the law?"

"Yes, I do! Right this minute! A traveler had car trouble near my house. Ray isn't here so it's only my father and me. Oh, I meant to ask. The trial here a few days ago? Was there ever a decision on that?"

"Darcy, is he at YOUR place?"

"Yes, George! How kind of you to offer! She needs to get to Norman this afternoon. How nice of you! Certainly is neighborly! May I tell her you'll be along?"

"On my way! Be right there!"

Darcy returned to the den smiling cheerfully. "I was just in the nick of time! Barely caught him on his way out the door. Five minutes more and I would have missed him! He'll be right here. He can drop you at the airport or drive you to Norman. By the way, it's a one-hour ride to Norman. Would you like to freshen up a bit? The powder room is just across the hall. Let me show you. Come along, Dear, this way."

The woman rose to docilely follow Darcy along the hall. Darcy opened the door to the powder room and waited while the stranger walked inside. She quietly shut the door and then barricaded it with a chair under the door knob. She raced back to the den to grab James by his arm.

"Sh-h-h! Dad! Shhhhh! Don't ask questions! Come with me! Shh! Breathe through thy nose! "

She whispered coaxingly as she steered him through the kitchen and out the back door. For once, James did not jump in to take charge. Meekly as a puppy, he let Darcy lead him from the house. She hurried him out the kitchen door into the garage, coaxing as they sped along.

"Hurry, Dad! Into my car! We cannot stay here! Shhh! A monster is locked in our bathroom! Shhhhhh! Get in the car! We have to go! The sheriff will be here any minute! We don't want to be in a shoot-out!"

With her father safely in the car, she left the garage and turned into the road leading to town. A couple of miles later, she saw the sheriff's car approaching and stopped to wave at him. As he drew near, she called,

"George, it's the Henderson boy! He's dressed as a woman but I recognized him! He's locked in my downstairs bathroom! He's all yours!" she shuddered.

"Good Lord! I left the house long enough to see if my cattle are still standing! Less than an hour! Do you mean the two of you got tangled up with Hank Henderson? You captured him? Wasn't he armed?"

"Ray, he was dressed as a woman, complete with wig and pantyhose. He thought his disguise was working and he didn't want to tip us off by getting rough."

"How did you know who he was? How did he get in here? I told both of you to keep the front door locked. I said-- Don't open the door to strangers!

James spoke first. "Ray, I wanted a short walk on the county road in front of the house. I only went a few steps to come across a car with a flat tire and a young woman looking in the trunk for a spare. She asked to use our phone to get help. I confess, I was taken in. I brought her, uh, him in."

"Like I said, they always manage to get in by divide-and-conquer tactics. And where were you, Darcy?"

"Ray, housework goes on, regardless of weather, escaped convicts, whatever! I went to the kitchen about lunch. I never heard Dad leave or I would have stopped him."

James tried his best to look innocent as Darcy went on. "Dad, I have to know! How in the world did you come across him? You were in the den with a newspaper and TV! Next I knew, you sailed through the front door with a fugitive in tow! Fill in the blanks for me. What happened?"

James bristled defensively as he growled,"After Ray left, I got restless. I've been penned in this house like an old pussy cat for a week! I'm sick of it! I wanted out so I decided to take a short walk on the road in front of the house. It's only a county road with local traffic. When I saw the woman, I only meant to bring her to the phone. I had no idea all Hell would break loose!" Shaking his head sadly, "Tsk! Tsk! I've always had an eye for the ladies! I must be getting old! Darcy, how did you catch on to his disguise?"

"His eyes! The coldest eyes I've ever seen! After I saw him at the trial, I knew I could never forget them. Though it took a moment to register, with his disguise to confuse me."

"Did he have a gun?"

"He had one but never used it. He thought his disguise was working. I think he wanted to leave quietly and not attract attention.

He had hope of getting away so he focused on that. If he pulled a gun and took a car, he'd be right back where he started, with state troopers after him."

Shaking his head in weary disbelief, Ray moaned, "It's all my fault! I should never have turned my back on the two of you."

"Ray, it was the best plan after all. If he found you here, he may have used his gun. When he found only an older man and a woman, he let his guard down. Please don't feel bad. Be thankful that we all came though it safely and we still have each other."

Chapter Thirty-Seven

The man paced back and forth in front of the bank. Peering at the empty street, he mused, looks like rain. At that moment, the blind was opened, the door unlocked. The clock on the bank wall showed exactly nine o'clock. He checked the street once more to see it still empty. He breathed a sigh of thanks and opened the door. Inside, he stood a brief moment as he looked about. Nothing like a good plan!

He took a deep breath as he approached a woman at a desk near the vault. "I need to use my safety box in the vault."

He showed his key with the identifying number. She smiled graciously as she selected the matching key from a drawer. She rose to lead him into the room that housed the vault. She took his key, along with hers, and as she turned to open the drawer, he wrapped an arm around her waist and said, "I have a gun! I want that crooked banker in here! I know you have a cell phone on your belt! Call him now! Don't mention me! Make up an excuse to get him in here!"

Darcy had driven into town early, thinking to finish errands and be home in time to start lunch. Ray needed an item from the implement dealer but hated to take time from his work to get it. "I have errands anyway. I can pick it up for you. How soon do you need it?"

"I needed it yesterday but I can manage til you get back. The weatherman said possible showers. I want to get that field finished before it rains. Thanks, Sweetheart!"

He grinned in appreciation and kissed her on his way out the kitchen door.

After purchasing the item for Ray, she stopped at the market. Instead of the quick in-and-out trip she planned, she ran into Minnie and Mo in the store. They were excited about a recent trip to Disney World and insisted on relating all the details, item by item. Darcy listened patiently until she saw an avenue for escape. After all, Ray was waiting for that part.

She made her way out of the store to be greeted by an angry sky. She stopped in her tracks, appalled at dark, murky clouds swirling in the west but rapidly moving closer.

"I never saw so many shades of dark blue in a cloud or that nasty shade of dark green. I wonder if I can make it home before that thing hits," she thought as she reached for her door handle. At that moment, wind, rain, and debris struck her forcefully. Nearby, a siren sounded.

Changing her course, she turned and raced toward the bank, the sturdiest building in town. She quietly pushed open a heavy door operated by air hinges to enter an empty bank. Leaning against the door, she stared at empty teller cages. Glass-enclosed offices at the rear were empty. A glance at the clock showed the bank had been open only ten minutes.

"I know! They heard the siren and took shelter in the vault! Not a bad idea!" she mused gratefully, racing in her sneakers toward the door to the vault.

The sight would remain stamped indelibly on her memory. The white-faced, trembling women were the first thing she saw. An obvious reaction to an approaching tornado. I wonder if my face is as white as theirs. Hmm! Wonder why they left the door wide open. Looks like they would close it part way to deflect flying debris.

"Move over, folks! Let a country girl in here! This looks like a real trash-mover." Laughing, Darcy inserted herself into the mass of bodies crowded into the space. Strained silence greeted her. An unbroken silence that dragged on, giving her an eerie feeling.

She looked around, thinking, "Did I say something wrong? Why do they stare at me? I feel like a party crasher!"

At that moment, Ethel Mae Praether moved enough to allow Darcy to see Fred Jenson and another man, a stranger. Fred's usually flabby, florid face looked exactly like bread dough. And the stranger held a gun in Fred's back.

"Good Lord, Darcy! You interrupted a bank robbery?"

"That's what I'm trying to tell you! I was running for my life to find shelter from a tornado, and I ran right into the middle of a robbery. The man with a gun in Fred Jenson's back said he would shoot anyone who moved. The women were scared stiff, too scared to cry, afraid to breathe.

"The man read about that scrape when the boys tried to steal that old safe. He decided this town was small enough to be an ideal target. He rented a deposit box and waited a few days while he watched. You could say he cased the joint. He got them all into the vault and he demanded money, lots of it, canvas bags full of it!

"That vault was so crowded, it was worse than an overloaded elevator. I knew he could not possibly watch all of us. I was the last one in, just inside the door, behind everyone else. After I got there, he sent one woman to fill some bags with large bills. When he turned to watch her, I reached over and pulled the door shut."

"What! You locked the vault? You locked yourself in with the bank robber?"

"Of course! We had no weapons, no way to call for help! The women were all too scared to move! Somebody had to do something!"

"Weren't you scared stiff?"

"Well, of course I was! I also knew he could shoot all of us, lock the vault on his way out, and be miles away before anyone noticed. He had the storm to distract everybody. I made up my mind! I would be like my pioneer grandmothers. I would not be a rabbit waiting for slaughter! I would die with my boots on!"

"Oh, Honey, don't even mention that! What did the robber do when the door closed him in?"

"It took him a minute to realize what happened. The vault is so well-built, so precise, the door so well-balanced, it was easy to pull it closed. It only made a tiny little click. He stood looking all around, wondering where the click came from. I thought about telling him it was Fred's dentures. That man was a basket case, teeth chattering, sweat rolling like rain. He's only good at robbing women. No good in a crisis."

"What did the man do?"

"He panicked! He realized he was trapped in there with us and he lost it! He got angry and threatened to shoot who did it. Only thing, they were all busy staring at the robber. Nobody knew who did it. If he shot one, he had to shoot us all, to be rid of witnesses."

"You were the only non-employ there! I can't believe they didn't give you up as sacrificial goat."

"Like I said, it was no good. If he shot one, he had to shoot us all. Then he'd be trapped with us! I doubt he wanted to be trapped in that small space for hours with fifteen dead bodies!"

"I have to know! Cut to the chase! Tell, for heaven's sake! Who got up the nerve to hit the alarm button?"

"Actually, nobody. Not intentionally. When Fred saw we were trapped, he told us the vault was set on time release. It would be tomorrow before it opened. It's air conditioned during banking hours, so there was no problem of air right then. We didn't know how bad the tornado was. It could be hours before someone noticed the bank. Probably everyone would think we took shelter somewhere else and would return any minute.

"While we digested that bit of news, Fred passed out! For once in his life, he did something decent for the good of mankind. He fainted! Without a word, he slowly closed his eyes and toppled back against the robber. That knocked the gun out of his hand! It hit the floor right between Ethel Mae's feet. She reacted like an old soccer player and kicked it toward the front of the vault, between all those feet, to stop at my feet! At that moment, Fred completed his swan dive. He slumped forward, then on the way down, he bumped the alarm button with his forehead. While all that was happening, I reached down and grabbed the gun.

"That's when the robber gave up. By the time George found someone to open the vault door, the robber was as anxious as the rest of us to get out of there! He gave no trouble when they took him away in handcuffs. He said he should have known better than to rob Toonerville. He said he saw more clowns here than at the circus. George said bank robbery is federal so they will hold him until a Marshall picks him up."

"What about Fred? Did he recognize your part in foiling the robbery of his precious bank? He should give you a reward!"

"I don't know. We tried to rouse him but he was out. We thought he hit his head when he fell. As soon as they got us out of there, an ambulance took him to the hospital. I didn't hang around to find out. I was worried about you so I hurried right home."

Ray wrapped his arms around his wife to clasp her close to him and buried his face in her hair.

"Darcy, with all that was going on, you worried about me?"

"Of course! Sitting up on that tractor makes you an obvious target for lightning."

"I work out in the open where I can see everything. When I saw that monster cloud, I raced with it to the house and got here just as it hit! I came inside and paced the floor while I watched the window, hoping to see you drive in. At the same time, I hoped you were inside in a safe place."

The phone broke the emotional moment. Freeing one arm, Ray responded to listen intently a moment before replacing the receiver.

"Darcy, you won't believe this! Ethel Mae from the bank said Fred Jenson is dead! She followed the ambulance to the hospital and waited. He has no close relatives so she stayed. She said she didn't feel right to leave him like that.

"He wasn't in a faint! He was dead on arrival! The doctor said he had a heart attack. It wasn't his first but this one was brought on by fright. The man was scared to death!"

"He was trying to jump my claim to this property. Now what happens about that?"

James entered from the hall to join in, "Yes, indeed, I want to know! Now what happens?"

"Dad, you were eavesdropping!"

James bristled with indignation as he declared, "Of course I was!

How else can I ever learn anything useful or interesting?'

"Then you know the banker who held that claim on my deed is dead?"

"Yes, and I have mixed emotions about that. I'm relieved that he is gone but I did look forward to destroying him. Thinking about it kept my blood circulating! In the Roaring Twenties, gangsters called it 'rubbing out.' Now, they say 'erasing.' I wanted to erase him! Every time I thought of all the grief he gave my little girl, I could hardly wait to do him in! I had some really clever ways planned. One of those unsolved things! I wanted to make him disappear down an old mine shaft! Even better, down a bat cave, with all the droppings! How appropriate!"

"Dad, you're too old and too frail to get into that! It might turn out the way Fred did. He collapsed and died on the spot! You don't want to go like that, do you?"

Her sermon merited a belligerent glare and a forward thrust of the lower jaw. "If I got caught, my plea would be senile dementia. They would send me to a state hospital. I could have a field day! I could plague my psychiatrist, confuse him on a weekly basis. Pester the nurses daily! They would vote unanimously to release me, to get rid of me!"

"Dad, you really are an old pirate! A charming one but a pirate, first, last and always."

Shaking his head and chuckling roguishly, he replied, "Can't help it! Comes down with the genes. We had a lot of pirates in our family. They all died rich. Can't find fault with that!"

He interrupted himself with roars of laughter. When he quieted, he reached for her hand, saying, "Now, Daughter, sit down. You and I need to talk. I meant to wait til after the land hearing but I'm betting it will be dropped. I meant to offer you a consolation prize if they took this farm away from you. I want to tell you while we are both well and sane. Sit down and listen! I will say this only once."

"Well, sure, Dad. Let's sit here on the couch. Is it alright for Ray to stay?"

"Of course! Ray is like my own. Now both of you, listen up!

Remember I told you about owning the gambling casino in Alaska?"

"Yes. You said you liked it but you got tired of it."

"I said that after I ran it for years, I got tired of it. I also said I ran it for years and it was better than a gold mine! I lived well but there was no way I could spend all I made. I played around in the stock market and that turned out well. Now I have left a token amount to the older girls but the bulk of it goes to you, Darcy. I know you will use it to improve this farm or you will use your time and money helping those who need it. Either one will suit me.

"Darcy, something else. You were right when you said I'm getting old and frail. I have a heart condition that could take me any moment. I must stay in touch with my doctor and keep my pace maker monitored, or I'm in deep trouble.

"I did not mean to come back and settle in here. I meant to stay a couple of days, long enough to see my daughters, with a long last look at this place. Then I would move on to die in a strange place. Truth is, you made me so comfortable and happy, I couldn't bear to leave. I hope, with all my being, that I am not a burden!

"All the time I was in Alaska, I thought about this place. It always seemed like my home. Plain truth is, I was homesick. I didn't know how much until I actually saw this place. And then I saw you! I only want to live out my days here and be buried next to Sarah. Can you handle that?"

"Of course, Dad! I wouldn't have it any other way! I'm grateful to get acquainted with you. It helps me to understand things that were a mystery as I grew up. I would grieve if you left now, after we've grown close. This was your home before it was ever mine. It's your home as long as you want!"

James, dark eyes dancing, looked long and hard at his daughter before he chuckled.

"Dad! Did I say something funny?"

"Not a thing! Not one thing! That last sentence you spoke is typical of you and your personality. I just told you I leave you a fortune and you didn't even ask the amount. Most women would be undone with curiosity. You think of others."

Ray had remained silent as long as he could. Laughing, he said "James, Darcy may not think this is funny but I can't be still. She thought you were like those homeless people we read about. You know, the kind who live out of their car and move about so the law won't pick them up?"

"Did she now? Darcy, you thought I was street people?"

"James, you arrived here in a new Cadillac and she thought you were a vagrant!" Ray chuckled.

Darcy laughed. "He ran a casino. He could have taken that car from a heavy loser or won it in a crap game."

"You thought I was a vagrant, yet you took me in? Come to think of it, you were right. I was homeless! Now that I am settled in, I can't think of any place I had rather live. I still think it's hilarious that you're not inquisitive about my net worth. Typical but laughable. I told you I'm leaving you a fortune and you don't blink an eye. The women I know would not sleep until they knew the amount."

"Dad, I think it's great that you want me to have it but I would never ask the amount. I don't even care how much! That is your business. The fact that you want me to have it is all that matters. I am touched!"

A flash of intuition raced through her mind. She blurted, "You're the anonymous donor to the Nelda Cole fund! I know it was you! Nobody in town knew so it must have been you!"

His mischievous grin was an admission.

"Since you're not interested in my money, you may wait until my will is read. I will add one more stipulation. There will be no formal gathering to read my will. Those things breed trouble and discontent. Each of you will be contacted by an attorney who will reveal only how much you received. Now, young lady, if you tell the other girls how much you received and they suffer from an attack of sibling rivalry, you can live with it! One other thing I can give you. My motto, 'Breathe through thy nose!'"

The telephone broke the sentimental moment. Darcy

responded, to hear, "Darcy, Ethel Mae Praether. After I called, I remembered the lawsuit about that old oil lease. I did a lot of work for Fred, mostly as a favor to him. He gave me a job when I got out of school and I will always be grateful to him. I helped him type and file and sort out his investments. I even became a notary public so it would save him money. Oh, how that man cut corners!

"I thought about that old lease and wanted to read it one more time. Funny thing! I searched this office all over and it's not to be found! I know he kept it in a drawer in his desk but it's not there! I thought you might sleep a little better tonight if you knew."

"Ethel Mae, I don't understand! Are you telling me the original paper disappeared? How can that be? Weren't there copies somewhere? Did he put it in a safety deposit box?"

"Darcy, listen closely. We, I mean all of us who were locked in that vault with a bank robber, we will always be grateful to you. Grateful for the neat way you got us out of there with no injuries. That was the cleverest thing anybody could have done! We talked it over and we tried to think of a way to thank you. We wanted to do something to show our genuine appreciation. So I thought about that old lease. You never talked about it but I know it's been a problem for you. Surprise! Surprise! It has disappeared! Like it should have years ago! It's gone and there were no copies. Fred had no relatives, no one to leave his estate to. I often wondered why he wanted to grab that land when he had nobody to leave it to. Maybe to prove to himself how smart he was. With no relatives, there is no one to pry into his papers. Most of his estate goes to charity. Now this conversation never took place! Do you understand what I am saying?"

"Ethel Mae, if ever you need anything, just ask. Since this conversation never took place, I should hang up, but not before I say 'Thank You!'"

Breathing a deep sigh of relief, she turned to say,

"Ethel Mae says the lease paper that caused all the controversy has disappeared. She looked all over and it cannot be found. And we are not to repeat any of this to anybody. It never happened. Do you hear me, Dad?

"Yep! I can breathe through my nose! My best trick! How about the rest of you!"

Ray burst out, "There is no lease paper? That means no hearing, no court fight! We're home free!"

Darcy looked fondly at each of the men beside her on the sofa. Ray's eyes had lost that clouded look brought about by worry. His face had returned to its natural smile. He looked like a kid who had just seen Santa Claus. James had a rapt look of one listening to soft music. She grasped a hand of each man. "Yes! We are home! Where we belong! Right where we want to be! We are home to stay!"

Printed in the United States
89438LV00001B/52-99/A